To Dylan and Maxwell,
brother-adventurers for a brave new century

★ CONTENTS ★

THE ABERNATHY BOYS

Believe It or Not . . .

. . . the adventures of Bud and Temple Abernathy are true.

As the boys journeyed nearly one hundred years ago, as they grew up, and as they grew old, they told many of their stories to reporters, strangers, and members of their own family, some of whom wrote down what they heard or took their photographs. To these people I am heartily grateful.

The bits of information that have been passed down are like a fistful of puzzle pieces scattered across a big blank tabletop. They show the basic facts of where the boys went and some of what they encountered and how they looked at the time of their travels. They even reveal hints of their character. But the picture is incomplete. Just about everything else that you'd want to know is left blank.

It's very important to say whether a book is fiction or

nonfiction, so that librarians know which shelf to put it on. Therefore, I must admit that in writing the Abernathy boys' stories I've used my imagination to fill in much of that blankness. Enough of it that we'll have to call this book fiction. Almost all of the basic facts that I could find about Bud and Temple are here in these pages, but I've woven them together with make-believe.

I tried not to make anything up out of thin air, however. Guided by that smattering of fact, I got in a car and traced the boys' steps. I quickly realized, though, that most of those steps have been paved over by highway. America looks some—but not much—like it did when the boys and their horses meandered across it. So I got to reading.

I read books about the olden days; about animals that were likely to have scampered or slithered across their path; about all the famous or semifamous people I knew they met and some I thought they might have met; about towns (now ghost towns) where folks were kind to them; about cowboys and cowboy ways of doing things, and so on. Finally, when I'd begun to see the world they lived in, it wasn't long before the boys seemed as real to me as I seem to myself.

Bud and Temple were such remarkably adventurous and brave boys, though, that no matter what I say you still may find it difficult to believe that their adventures really happened. After all, they belonged to a world that is no longer there and can only be seen in the mind, by unimagining the last one hundred years.

For starters you'd have to peel all those paved roads and highways from the land. No driver's licenses, no stoplights, no traffic cops.

Noises we hardly even notice anymore—the semi truck barreling down the interstate, the overhead hum of the jet— would have to be hushed. Then uninvent the computer, the television, the radio, antibiotics, seedless blueberries, plastic, video games, and countless other things that you probably can't imagine living without.

Once you'd erased all that the twentieth century added to the world, you'd have to put back what it took away. Where now there are shopping malls, crowd the land with trees, more than you think will fit, or flood it and make marshes, or fill it with nothing at all but nothingness.

Swell the populations of birds, fish, and mammals, and be generous about it. Return the prairie dogs and their prairie dog towns and their prairies at once. And don't forget the "loafers," a.k.a. the "lobos"—I mean the *wolves*. Now add the danger that is the dark side of nature. The land wasn't nearly as primitive back in 1909, when these journeys begin, as it was in 1809, let alone 1709, but it was still free enough for real adventure.

Now imagine, smack in the middle of it, two boys—one nine, one five—on two white horses. And try to believe that they would, with all their hearts and all their courage, want to see it with their own eyes before the twentieth century made it vanish.

★ ONE ★
The Caprock

Toward the end of the nineteenth century, when a few parts of the West were still hanging on to their ancient wide-open wildness, Jack Abernathy decided to journey to the caprock. He was only fifteen then.

It was a rare sort of boy who was drawn to that place in those days. After eight years' riding trail and busting broncos for outfits in and around Sweetwater, Texas, Jack was already a seasoned cowboy. He was restless. He was spindly and tough and hungry for the sort of adventure a young fellow could never find if he always stayed close to home and his loving family.

He was after that wildness that the old West was famous for, and he was willing to chase it all the way into one of the most frightful places on earth, where the wind was fierce, the water was foul, and even the mirages were mean-tempered. And he was willing to go there alone.

The caprock rises like a giant's porch out of the low Texas plains and spreads yawningly westward till—after what may seem like an eternity—it hits the Rocky Mountains. It goes by a few other names too, none of which is "holiday haven" or "vacation paradise." Just about the nicest thing anyone has called it is "the staked plains," and even that sounds better in Spanish—*el llano estacado*. As a getting-away place, it's no Coney Island.

Early explorers put it down on their maps as the "Great American Desert" and described it in woeful tales as the loneliest region on earth. The caprock seemed to them as vast as the sea and more terrible, with no beginning and no end and only misery to write home about.

But that was just one way of looking at it. Many of the Comanche Indians, who for a long time reigned supreme there, might have had a much different opinion. Just as there are people who eagerly choose a life at sea, there are others who are drawn by deep desire to the boundless, uncrowded places of the earth, of which the caprock is one of the most wondrous examples. Generally this has been the sort of person who chooses freedom over safety and adventure over comfort. In short, the very sort that was an Abernathy.

Riding into the wind, past some of the last remaining herds of buffalo, past antelope and white-winged doves, toward a distant horizon that never seemed to get any closer, Jack eventually arrived at the caprock ranch of Colonel Charles Goodnight and asked for a job.

Colonel Goodnight was a legend among cattlemen and, like the caprock itself, bigger than life. He was a man of few words and quick decision. "Abernathy," he said at their first meeting, "it's plain that you're a mite crazy." Then he gave him just about the highest compliment of the West: "But I reckon you'll do to ride the river with."

After proving himself by gentling hundreds of Goodnight's meanest broncos, Jack asked for a more dangerous job, something that would take him right into the heart and jaws of the Wild West. The colonel squeezed some tobacco juice through his teeth and gave his head a good scratching, and then he decided to let Jack try his hand at hunting wolves.

Wolves had a nasty habit of preying on cattle and were a menace to ranchers. They'd been shot, trapped, hamstrung, lassoed, hooked, pierced, and poisoned till they'd all but disappeared from most of the country. The caprock was one of the few places left where they were still abundant.

Jack took to his new profession like he was born for it and soon discovered a daredevil way to catch live wolves with his bare hands, earning a bit of fame and the nickname "Catch 'Em Alive" Jack. Whenever a wild animal leaped into his path, he never flinched or failed to tame it. Fear was something he never knew.

"Jack Abernathy," his mother always told him on those occasions when he went home to see her, "you surely won't die with your boots off."

By the time he was seventeen Jack had escaped disaster so many times that the risk of death no longer scared or thrilled him. His boots were worn thin, and so was his spirit. He was a brave boy, but he was only human. The loneliness of the caprock had begun to wear him down.

Stalking the plains for wolves one day, he asked his horse: "Is there more to life than mesquite and lobo scat?" Who else could he ask? There was nobody else around for miles and miles and miles, and his horse was an excellent listener.

He felt a powerful need to find out. And so it was that at seventeen, Jack bought himself a pair of patent leather shoes and a derby hat, packed his cowboy gear up in a trunk, said good-bye to his horse and the caprock, and headed by train to the Patterson Institute of Music in Hillsboro, Texas, where he enrolled as a classical piano student. It was there, to his great surprise, that he met the love of his life, Miss Jessie Pearl Jordan, the schoolmaster's sixteen-year-old niece.

Pearlie was an orphan. Like Jack, she'd grown old before her time. As soon as they met, the two teens wished they could have kept each other company always. They felt like children again. They vowed to stay together till death.

Pearlie's uncle refused to grant them his permission to marry. So Jack kidnapped her, and they became husband and wife before anyone could stop them. Loneliness was behind them forever, and so were Jack's musical aspirations.

They wanted a big family and wasted no time getting started. The young couple soon had a baby girl named Kitty Joe, and then they had another, called Goldie. Then, in the year 1900, at the dawning of the twentieth century, they had a son whom they named Louis, though they almost always called him Bud.

"We'll keep him safe," Pearlie said. In her mind she saw Bud growing strong and healthy and staying close to home, close to his parents, who would never abandon him, never fail to protect him, and, she prayed, not die before he'd become a man.

"He'll always feel free," said Jack. In his mind he saw his son following in his own footsteps, seeking adventure and open spaces, and fearing nothing.

The truth was, however, that the kind of boy Bud would become wasn't entirely up to either one of them. Whether, for instance, he'd become the sort to long for the caprock's freedom or to prefer the safety of home was in the end entirely up to Bud.

★ **TWO** ★
Crossroads

Before Bud was born, his family moved to a patch of prairie in that middle part of America now known as Oklahoma, where the East runs smack into the West. They grazed a small herd of cattle and lived in a tiny house built out of a piano crate.

Upon the piano itself, which took up most of the parlor, sat an old wooden mantel clock that had belonged to Pearlie's dear departed mother and was the one thing she had to remember her by. Its gentle tick-tocking lulled baby Bud to sleep each night and was a comfort to one and all.

It was a ramshackle little homestead, but it sat in the midst of a newly settled land so vast that merely to breathe the air made tiny Bud feel like a giant. His parents were very poor, but Bud never knew it. He didn't have a complaint in the world and quickly grew strong and clever.

They called their homestead "Cross Roads," because the county's only two roads crossed at a point just beyond the hill that rose above the stream that ran past the stand of cotton-woods on the westernmost edge of their land. To Bud it felt like the crossroads of the world, leading everywhere, leading anywhere.

Most every night, when darkness fell on the prairie, Bud and the girls gathered around a coal-oil lamp and listened to their father's stories of his youth on the caprock. It was the stories more than the lamp that seemed to brighten the black night.

They were stories of near-death and desolation, but to Bud they were pure delight. Even when he was too little to under-stand every word, he got the gist. The caprock was a world that made his own life at Cross Roads seem tame and pale. Every hardship his father endured seemed to Bud like heaven on earth, and every calamity was the height of glamour.

Bud's father filled his tales with fascinating people—cowboys and hunters and the great, bow-legged giant, Charles Goodnight. He stuffed them with fantastic animals—antelopes, wolves, the last living buffaloes, tarantulas, and centipedes. The star of the show was often the giant vinegar-roon, a disgusting caprock creature that he described as "the deadliest reptile on the range." In true fact, however, the vine-garroon wasn't a reptile at all. It was actually a kind of whip-scorpion, but Bud didn't know that then, nor did he care to know.

With his hands wriggling in all directions, Bud's father depicted the beast: "Eight eyes, six legs, two pincers armed with lethal blades, a mighty tail like a whip, a back like a conquistador's armor, and a vinegary-smelling venom as poisonous as arsenic."

In his mind Bud saw a frightful monster. He never let his daddy see his fear, though, nor did he let it stop him from yearning for the day when he could have his own adventures on the caprock. The mantel clock never missed a beat, but it couldn't tick fast enough for Bud.

★ THREE ★
Lone Wolf

Like the prairie dogs, the coyotes, the dung beetles, the burrowing owls, the jackrabbits, the fork-tailed flycatchers, the ravens, and the hawks, Bud took naturally to life at Cross Roads.

He was always a bit small for his age, but he was uncommonly strong and independent. After being born, the first thing he taught himself was how not to cry when he was sad. Next he wasted no time in figuring out what a spoon was for and how to use it. He was the kind of boy who liked to do things without anybody's help. He didn't like to bother people. He rarely asked for anything. Though he had his two older sisters, he preferred to play by himself. His mother called him a "lone wolf."

When he was two, his younger sister Johnny was born. At

that early age Bud had already learned to walk and talk and run and throw a rope cleanly around the neck of Catch, the family dog, who gladly stood in for a frisky calf. At three he was already calculating how to get up on a horse without a boost from his father.

Johnny was a born tomboy. Even as a baby, she'd rattle the bars of her crib and scream to be let out to play with Bud. "Bud" was her first word, and she used it often. Bud was a dreamy kind of boy, though, and his eyes were always gazing out toward the open pasture, where he was aching to be. He didn't mean to, but the true fact was that he usually looked right past her.

When he was four, his little brother Temple was born. Temp was funny and spunky and antsier than a slice of watermelon on a picnic ground. He, too, idolized Bud, from the moment he laid his eyes on him. He couldn't help smiling ridiculously whenever Bud walked into a room. By then, however, Bud was becoming a fine little cowboy, and he had no time at all to play with babies. He usually ignored Temp, as he'd ignored Johnny, though he didn't do it on purpose. It was just that his mind was elsewhere.

Trotting around on a pony came even more easily to Bud than walking. When, with just a cluck of his tongue and a little pressure from his leg, he found that he could make the pony gallop, he felt he'd made the most incredible discovery in the world. Great distances disappeared beneath him in a flash.

Up in the saddle, he wasn't a boy but a steam engine. He never wanted to walk again, anywhere, not even to the privy.

Sometimes Jack would tack up Sam Bass, the handsome white Arabian who was his best wolf-hunting horse, and lift Bud into the saddle in front of him. Together they tended the herd. Bud pressed his cheek against Sam's silky neck and watched wispy clouds skimming across blue skies. He loved the feel of wind and the taste of dust. With his father's arms around him Bud had a warm, safe feeling that he found nowhere else.

Bud thought about Sam Bass all of the time, even when he was at home by the mantel clock. Sam was as fine a horse as he could imagine, and Bud wished he could be with him every tick-tocking minute of the day.

Step by step, lesson by lesson, the things that once were new and difficult for Bud became second nature. He learned how to smell the air for water, to read sign for trail, to map the stars, to shoot, to mend a saddle, to make a quirt, to build a campfire, and he learned three ways to kill a rattlesnake.

He picked up the cowboy way of talking. "Quirt" for whip. "Remuda" for a herd of cow horses. "Justins" or "mule ears" for boots. "Hair case" for hat. "Bronc squeezer," "heel squatter," "leather pounder," "puncher," "twister," and "saint" were some of the many ways Bud knew to say "cowboy." Bud did most of his talking to horses, though, so the words he used most were "giddap!" and "glang!," which, as every horse knew, meant "go!"

His father taught him all the rules of the ranch, range, and trail, and to value the "true fact" over the "fancy idea." He taught him to be confident, even when he was afraid. Bud tried to develop his own philosophies of life, too, as every boy must. It was hard work, but easier when he was riding Sam.

When he turned five, Bud was given a pony of his own, which he named Geronimo for the famous Apache warrior. Geronimo was smaller, stouter, slower, and not nearly as clever as Sam, and he was always stumbling on prairie dog holes. But his coat was white like Sam's, and he had potential. With patience, Bud trained him to be a pretty good cow pony.

When his daddy got a job as a deputy sheriff in a nearby town, Bud took charge of the livestock. Working made Bud feel needed and useful, and that made him happy. It also gave him the confidence he required to be brave like his father.

He and Geronimo spent long hours every day on their own. Ahead of them, there was nobody in sight except the cattle. Behind him, there was nothing but the puff of dust the pony kicked up and Catch the dog, who—tongue flapping, toes dancing—followed them everywhere.

It never seemed like work to Bud. He liked to pretend that he wasn't safe at home in Oklahoma but far away, out on the caprock. Not at Cross Roads, but on the famous Goodnight ranch, where his father had worked as a boy. Not amid tall, soft grasses and cottonwood trees, but among prickly pears and sagebrush. Not running with Catch—"part collie, part pussycat," his mother always said—but with wolves. Not on a homestead measured in acres, but a sealike desert so vast it's immeasurable.

It was always good to get home, though, at the end of the day. The sound of the mantel clock would at once make him feel sleepy and safe and calm. His mother would be readying supper with the girls. Temple would be on her hip, biting his lip and trying not to smile at the sight of his big brother. If Bud happened to notice him, Temp would blush from head to toe.

Many was the day when, seeing Bud come home in the evening, Pearlie would look up and forlornly say, "Louis Abernathy, you surely won't die with your boots off." He still had the pudgy cheeks and the pouty lips of a baby, but she plainly could see what kind of boy he was fast becoming.

"No, ma'am," he'd say. It pleased him no end to hear it. "I don't reckon I will."

★ FOUR ★
Temp

Temp was a plump little baby with a laugh that bubbled and popped like porridge in the pan. Whenever he crawled or toddled into a room, he'd be chased by one of the older girls, thrown to the floor, and tickled and pinched till he was gasping for breath and could take no more. Those girls just couldn't keep their hands off of him.

He looked the picture of a sweet little innocent thing, but in truth he was a daredevil and a danger to himself. He was always crawling in his diaper under the bellies of bulls or broncos, or chasing poisonous snakes and insects under rocks, or trying to climb up windmill towers. There were thousands of ways to get hurt out there at Cross Roads, and Temple learned them all in the first year and a half of his life. Pearlie had to hold on to him most of the time, just to keep him from scampering off and breaking himself.

If he could have talked, he would have explained that what he was scampering after was Bud. When he was crawling toward a bronco, it was in order somehow to get on its hard, hairy back and ride it out to where Bud was tending the herd. When he caught an insect, it was in order to show it to Bud. When he climbed up a windmill tower, he did so for the view he hoped it would provide—of Bud.

Being born four years too late to be Bud's best friend was Temp's only vexation in life. When Bud ignored him, he shriveled up inside. His only consolation—his solace and joy—was the pursuit of insects. From an extremely early age, Temp had an uncanny ability to catch them and to understand the way their minds worked. When he couldn't play with Bud, he busied himself with a bug.

When it came time to learn to walk, Temp wasn't satisfied till he'd learned to walk just like Bud, ever so slightly pigeon-toed. When it was time to learn to talk, he started with the last words he'd heard Bud say. Therefore, his first word wasn't "mama" but "glang." Then came "giddap." For a long time he used "glang" and "giddap" to mean just about everything.

One Sunday, long before Temp had even turned two, Johnny put one of Bud's old Stetson-style hair cases on him, tied a red bandanna around his neck, plopped his feet into a pair of oversized mule ears, and planted a little quirt in his fist.

Dressed up like that, Temp looked like a baby-doll cowboy. When the rest of the family caught sight of him, they all laughed till they couldn't breathe and decided it might be funny to see what he looked like sitting atop Sam Bass.

By then the Stetson hat, which was about five sizes too big, had slipped down over Temp's eyes. He could see nothing but his own two feet. When he felt his daddy grabbing him by the ribs and sensed himself being lifted up—higher than a hip, higher than a high chair, higher than he'd ever been lifted before—he still couldn't guess where he was going.

Then, suddenly, he saw Sam's soft white neck twitching below him and felt himself teetering in the saddle. He pushed the hat back off his eyes, and where he was became wonderfully clear. He squealed with sheer delight, gripped Sam's mane in one pudgy little hand, quirted him with the other, and he cried, "Glang! Giddap!"

Everyone fell to pieces laughing. In slapping his knee, Jack accidentally let go of the reins, just as Temp let loose a "giddap" that had just enough confidence in it to get Sam trotting. Before anyone knew what had happened, Temp and Sam had disappeared behind the house.

Bud was the first to catch up with them. "Whoa!" Bud hollered, whereupon Sam stopped dead in his tracks. When Temp turned around and saw an expression of worry on his brother's face such as he'd never seen before, he blushed from head to toe. Then the ill-fitting boots slipped off his feet, and he fell out of the saddle into a pot of geraniums.

"Whoa" became his third word, and not a moment too soon.

That night, after all the children had been tucked into their beds and there was no sound in the house but the tick-tocking of the mantel clock, Bud lay on his back awake. Temp lay awake, too, watching his brother through the soaring bars of his crib.

Bud's hands were folded beneath his head, and his eyes were tracing a crooked line across the ceiling. Temp knew without being told that there were more than cracks on that ceiling. He knew that Bud was off on an imaginary adventure in a distant world, bigger and more exciting than Cross Roads. Temp had a way of believing Bud's dreams and fantasies, just as he believed that the cattle, the windmills, and all the bugs were real. He wanted to say something to him, but all he could think to say was "Glang, giddap, whoa," and that didn't seem appropriate.

He lay on his back, clutching Bud's old Stetson hat, and searched the ceiling. If only Bud would tell him where he was going up there! Then Temp could go with him! He would follow him anywhere. He couldn't bear it if Bud left him behind. Soon, though, he'd spotted a hairy spider, and he fell asleep hoping it would drop into his hand on a thread of silk.

★ **FIVE** ★

Jack Catches a Big One

The beginning of the twentieth century was a very good time to be alive if you were an adventurer. Daring acts were in general cheered, making heroes out of the men who performed them. And no one cheered more loudly than the president of the United States.

President Theodore Roosevelt was a lover of the West, the rough, the tough, the outdoorsy, and the bold. He believed that the "strenuous life" was the best life, and he deplored anyone who was lazy or fearful or shied away from danger.

If there was someone somewhere doing something audacious, brave, risky, intrepid, daring, or even a little crazy, he wanted to know about it. When a friend from Oklahoma told him about "Catch 'Em Alive" Jack Abernathy, a deputy sheriff who made extra money by catching live wolves with his bare hands and selling them for $50 to zoos and circuses, he made it his business to learn more. That meant seeing it for himself. So he got on a train to Oklahoma and spent five days on a hunt with Jack and Sam Bass and some friends. It was a momentous occasion in the lives of the Abernathys.

Jack would not disappoint. He caught a great many wolves with a prowess that dazzled his honored guest. Afterward, when Pearlie and the children met up with the hunting party, the president was still shaking his head in amazement. "That was bully!" he said. "That was as bully a thing as I've ever seen."

"Boooli," mimicked Temp. It was his fourth word.

That got everyone laughing, including the president. He swept Temp into his arms and said, "I don't know who I like better. The wolfer, his horse, his wife, or his kids."

Meeting President Roosevelt was the honor of a lifetime. Framed photographs of him went up on every wall of the piano-crate house. Shortly afterward, however, an even greater honor came Jack's way when he received a telegram from the president summoning him to Washington.

Jack's hands, usually so steady, trembled as he read. A week later, they were still shaking when, in his cowboy clothes, with a six-shooter strapped to his hip, he boarded the train for Washington. He was practically in a tizzy when, upon arriving in the capital, he walked straight to the White House and into the president's office—six-shooter and all—where he was given the biggest news of his life. President Roosevelt had decided to make him the United States Marshal for the terri-tory—soon to be state—of Oklahoma.

Back at Cross Roads a week later, Jack and Pearlie gathered the children together and told them to prepare themselves to be amazed. "Your daddy is going to be a very important man," Pearlie told them, as Jack's cheeks turned the color of straw-berry pop. He'd be earning plenty of money to give the chil-dren the things they deserved, she said. They were leaving the cracked walls of the piano-crate house and moving to a brand-new house in Guthrie, which was then the territorial capital.

There would be no more long days with the cattle for Bud. He'd be trading in his mule ears for school shoes.

As the girls squealed, Bud was shocked speechless. How could he get on without Geronimo? Without Sam Bass? When he found the strength to speak, his voice cracked as he begged, "Please let me stay. Please don't make me go." Bud had never before asked for anything. It stunned everyone to see him so desperate. Temp, for one, was distressed.

For Jack, Bud's misery was almost unbearable to behold. He was on the verge of agreeing to let him stay, when Pearlie put her foot down. "No, son," she said. "It's school for you, and games that children play, and a sturdy roof over your head, whether you like it or not."

Bud's face was ashen. He sputtered and stammered. "Now, now," said Pearlie, putting her arm around her oldest son. "Sam and Geronimo and Catch will come with us to Guthrie. We'll return to Cross Roads on all your school holidays. We'll leave Grandma's mantel clock here, just to prove to you that we'll always come back. I wouldn't leave that behind, would I? You'll see. We're all going to be so happy," she said, clutching Bud to her in a way that she hadn't done since he was a baby. She made it impossible for him to doubt her. "You're going to be happy, Louis Abernathy, just like all of us!"

★ SIX ★
Guthrie, OK

And happy they were indeed—for a while.

After all, Guthrie was an exciting, modern city. There were brick sidewalks, electric streetcars, and even an automobile in town, which belonged to the doctor. There was a modern fire station with horses that were exceptionally fast, and a big, clanging, busy train station with a Harvey House restaurant. There were no finer restaurants in all the West than the ones Mr. Fred Harvey built at stations along the Santa Fe railroad. And there could be no waitress anywhere more polite or pleasant than a Harvey Girl.

There was a constant flow, in and out, of people who carried about them the look and smell and dust of distant places. There were state politicians, and entertainers from far away, and prohibitionists. There were traveling salesmen, arriving every day by train, with their leather sample cases, their spiffy clothes, and their smooth talk. They were often telling jokes to shopkeepers, and it seemed to Bud that they floated about on clouds of laughter. Jack called them "drummers" in a way that sounded like an insult. But Bud thought they were fascinating.

Every day now, Bud snapped on a celluloid collar and cuffs and, with Catch following him all the way, took the streetcar to school. He sat at the back of the classroom beneath a banner that read "Faithful Study Succeeds," and he learned to spell and add and draw apples and cats under the critical eye of Miss Violet Irene Moore, his schoolteacher. His hand—so steady with a rope, so strong with a branding iron—shook terribly whenever she was watching.

Sitting there in the classroom, he appeared to be an ordinary six-year-old boy. No one could tell just by looking at him that he was capable of doing a grown man's work or that, when you got right down to it, he'd probably learned as much in his short life as his teacher had learned in hers.

Miss Moore certainly didn't seem to know. "Tsk-tsk," she'd say down her nose, as she hovered over him. "Mr. Abernathy, you can do much better, can't you, with that cat?"

That was the worst the teacher ever said to him, though. He never got in fights or made trouble. He didn't need to. Bud wasn't the biggest kid in school, and he wasn't the loudest. He was simply the strongest little kid in all of Guthrie. Everyone knew it, and nobody wanted to make him prove it.

He got himself a slingshot and some marbles and learned

to box by the Marquis of Queensbury rules. He became best friends with a boy his age named Dylan Bailey, who lived in the rich part of town called "Snob Hill." Bud had never had a friend like Dylan before.

On all the important topics of the day, Bud and Dylan were in complete agreement. Automobiles, for instance, were, in their opinion, "stink buggies" and would never take the place of horses. When they saw the doctor drive past in his sputtering black Ford, they would exchange disgusted looks that said volumes.

They rarely spoke, really, except occasionally to say, "What should we do now?"

"I dunno. What do you want to do?"

"I dunno. What do you want to do?"

And so on.

Eventually they'd get around to looking at maps of the West. Slowly they moved their fingers westward across the 98th meridian and the 100th meridian. They got to know every trail, every water sink, every ranch and train track that existed out on the caprock. They knew exactly where the Goodnight ranch was and how to get there from Guthrie.

They imagined sometimes that they were really there amid the sagebrush and the jackrabbits. And silently, without ever discussing it, they came to an understanding that someday— soon—they'd go there together.

Temple hated Dylan. He hated the very sight of him. It was nothing he did or said; there was no logic to Temp's hatred at all. The truth was that Dylan was a very friendly boy. Bud never noticed when Temple was there, lurking behind their backs while they were playing marbles on the floor. But Dylan always did. "Hey, Temp," he'd say, "why don't you pull up a marble and join us? C'mon, I'll teach you how to plump from the taw line." Still, Temple just plain hated him.

Temp considered himself the luckiest of all the Abernathy kids, because he alone got to share a bed with Bud every night, while the girls slept in a separate room. He was growing up, learning to talk and to do lots of the things Bud liked to do. But the truth was that the four years that separated them seemed to be getting wider all the time, and it didn't help matters at all to have Dylan getting between them.

Dylan had a little brother Temp's age named Maxwell. Temp's mother had high hopes that those two would become friends, but Temple didn't like him any better. Max would say something preposterous, like "Sam Bass is ugly." And Temp would say, "Come here and let me whoop you." Then the next thing you knew, Dylan was dragging Max home in tears.

Temp would stomp off to his room and pull Bud's old Stetson hat down over his ears, while he could hear his mother telling Bud, "Don't ignore your brother. Play with him sometimes. He's lonely."

Pearlie worried about her youngest son's loneliness so much that she'd gotten pregnant. In secret she told him that the new baby that was coming was a gift for him, so that he could have someone small to play with. She'd smile at him, take his chin in her hand, and she'd say, "But I'll *always* be your friend, boy. Come play with *me*."

Looking up at her then, Temp felt more kindly toward Dylan, whose mother mostly scolded him, and he allowed a tight grin to crack open his hard face. Gazing into her eyes he saw only happiness and not a single hint of the sadness that was soon to come.

SEVEN

The Least Bright Night

By Christmas of 1906, Pearlie's belly was beginning to grow round, and she was jollier than Santa. She created a frenzy around the house—cleaning, baking, decorating—all the while singing Christmas songs to her tummy and smiling in an exaggerated way that the children found peculiar.

When Jack gave her his Christmas present—a new brass mantel clock, with a statue of Napoleon on top—her eyes bulged with tears. She placed it atop the piano, saying, "It's perfect. Everything's perfect. It's a miracle." Then the tears began to spill.

These few drops were of deep concern to all of the children, who had never before seen their mother cry for any reason. Kitty Joe clutched the hand of Goldie, who grabbed the arm of Johnny, who squeezed the shoulder of Temp, who turned with great perplexity to Bud, who merely shrugged. They watched in suspense as a fat, quivering tear teetered on the tip of their mother's nose, and together they held their breath until, at last, it splashed onto her lap. A smile spread across her face and she boosted her nose upward, but Temp's brow still was twisted with worry. "Don't look at me like that," she said, taking his chin in her hand. "I'm *happy*, for goodness' sake. Can't you tell?"

By springtime, though, just when the children were growing accustomed to her strange new happiness, her mood changed again—abruptly, and for the worse. As she grew fatter, she grew weak and ill. It began to be difficult for her to cook and take care of the house. As May neared, she was so tired that she couldn't even stand up. Her fingers and feet were so swollen that she couldn't wiggle them. She couldn't fit into her boots anymore. The children tiptoed around her so as not to disturb her. They never saw her cry again, and yet they worried about her terribly.

One day in May, when she thought she was alone in the parlor with Bud, Pearlie said, "Oh, Louie, this baby will be the end of me." They weren't alone, though. Temple was hiding underneath the piano.

She saw fear spread across Bud's face, so she quickly added, "Don't worry, son, the baby will soon be born, and then it will be over. Now go and play with Temple, won't you?"

She grabbed Bud's hand. "Please," she said, "look after Temple. He needs you. Promise me."

She was never calmer than when something difficult was happening. And Bud had never seen her calmer than she was at that moment, which scared him. "Temp?" he asked nervously. "What's wrong with Temp?"

"Just promise me," said Pearlie.

"I promise," said Bud. "'Course I will."

When he left her, he looked for Temple in their room and in the barn and in the garden where he liked to play with dung beetles. He looked for him in just about every place, except for under the piano, where Temp stayed hiding for the rest of the afternoon, watching his mother for tears or other signs of sadness. Eventually, Bud had to give up looking. He got on Geronimo and rode over to Dylan's house.

The very next day, the doctor's stink buggy sputtered up to the barn, and an hour later the baby was born. She was a girl. Her great healthy lungs produced a whopping cry that seemed to shake the whole house. The children huddled together by the piano, waiting for their father to come out and hug them and to tell them the great news. But when finally he emerged from the bedroom, his face was pale and he wouldn't speak. He was a terrible sight to behold.

The doctor followed him out and told the children that their mother had succumbed to "Bright's Disease," which was a very nice name for something terrible called "consumption of the kidneys." Though he'd tried to save her, in the end it was her time to go. "Poor children," he said. "Who will look after you now?" Then he got in his stink buggy and sputtered away. The children hadn't understood a word he said, and yet they understood everything.

Silently, their daddy went out to the barn, fetched Sam, and rode off, thundering down the street and trailing a cloud of dust. He rode to the edge of town, where the dirt road faded into the open prairie, into which he disappeared for hours, galloping Sam till he hadn't an ounce of strength left in him.

When he came back late that night, there was no sound in the house but the ticking of the new mantel clock. He gasped when he saw all the children huddled together in the dark, waiting for him. It was as if he hadn't realized till then just how many children he had.

He lit a coal-oil lamp and gathered everyone around the piano, upon which sat the carefree clock. He held the new baby in his arms, and he said, "Your mama died with her boots off, children." Bud's heart ached to hear it. Temple clenched his jaw.

"This baby," their father said, "will be called Pearlie. That way she'll know her mother's name as well as her own." He briefly put his free hand on Bud's shoulder. The weight of it made Bud feel real loneliness for the first time in his life. Baby Pearlie began to bawl.

"You must be strong children and never cry," he said, shaking the baby as gently as his stiff arms would let him. "Your mother wouldn't like it. From now on, before you do *anything*, you must always ask yourself, 'What would Mother say?' You have to do this for yourselves," Jack said, raising his voice to be heard over the baby's sobs, "because I'm afraid I will never be able to do it for you. I will never be able to say or think or do anything so well or as sweetly as Pearlie."

★ EIGHT ★
Girls, Girls, Girls

This wailing of baby Pearlie was a great torment to Temp. He stared hard at her twisted face out of a desire to understand and soothe her misery, and, in so doing, took his mind off his own heartbreak, somewhat.

When she opened her eyes for the very first time, the person she saw was Temple. Like a newborn bird who attaches itself to the first creature it lays its eyes on, little Pearlie chose Temple to be her mother.

Pearlie cried all through her first night and all through the next night, too, as Temp rocked her cradle. She cried for the whole of the week and for most of the year. For the larger part of her second year she rarely stopped wailing, except to catch her breath. It was only Temple who could ever get her to stop, but only for a minute or two. As soon as he left the room, she'd begin again to cry.

When she turned two, she blew out the candles on her birthday cake and turned to Temp with a smile so bright and sweet and unexpected that it caused him nearly to fall over. From then on there were no more tears, and, everywhere that Temple went, little Pearlie followed. Shaking her was like side-stepping his own shadow.

On those rare occasions when Pearlie went down for a nap and Temp had a minute to himself—to look for Bud or hunt for bugs—one of the older girls would appear out of nowhere and stick to him like chewing gum.

Where once Temp had one mother, which was plenty, he now had three. Kitty Joe, Goldie, and Johnny all took turns telling him what to do and when to do it and, mostly, what *not* to do.

While their mother was there, they hadn't realized what a daredevil Temple was. They hadn't known, when Pearlie was alive to do it, what hard work it was keeping him in one piece. All the girls did now, it seemed to Temp, was say no. *Don't touch that. You'll hurt yourself!* The days of tackling and tickling and laughing till he turned purple were over. And Temple sorely missed them.

Bud was at school most of the time or else at Dylan's house, and Temp was counting the days till fall, when he, too, would at last become a student. He'd ride the streetcar with Bud to school, eat lunch right beside him, and never let him out of his sight. Till then, however, it was girls, girls, girls.

Whenever he could, Temp would jump at the chance to tag along with his father to the marshal's office, where he'd spend the day studying the Wanted posters. Among the sour, scraggly, mean-looking men lined up along the wall, there was one friendly face that always jumped out at him. He couldn't take his eyes off it. This one's name, Temple learned, was A.Z.Y. His daddy said that this badman was a fugitive from Arizona and much meaner than he looked. A.Z.Y. hated all lawmen, in particular Marshal Jack Abernathy, and had once tried to shoot him dead.

Temp had a hard time believing it, though. A.Z.Y. had long pale hair pulled back in a ponytail and a young, gentle face spread wide open in the biggest, most sparkling smile Temp had ever seen on an outlaw. It was hard to believe that a criminal could have teeth so white and shiny. He didn't look mean at all.

Temp's daddy said that A.Z.Y. had broken out of prison and was hiding out somewhere with his "brothers," which is what he called the band of misfits that were his gang. "He's probably rustling cattle or stealing horses out on the caprock," he said. "In which case, we'll never find him."

Temp knew it was wrong, but he envied A.Z.Y. Oh, to be out on the caprock with your brothers. Heck, Temp would take just one brother. In a wide-open space too big to be found in. With nobody telling you *No*. And nobody telling you where to go and nobody minding if you happened to hurt yourself a little.

★ NINE ★

Invisible Line

Temp was five now, which was getting pretty big, but Bud was nine, and that was a lot older. Guthrie didn't look the same through nine-year-old eyes as it had when Bud first saw it. It had lost its shine. Not even a meal at the Harvey House excited him much anymore. His celluloid collar was getting tight. His schoolwork didn't much interest him at all. The end of the school year was still a few weeks away, and already he was dreading the start of the next one.

Every day Bud would look out the classroom window and see Catch waiting for him patiently, and he'd think, *Catch, are you daft? There's no leash around your neck. Why don't you run?*

At home, he'd see Sam and Geronimo in the muddy little paddock behind the tiny barn, pawing at the fence, and he'd think, *Jump! Why don't you jump?*

Then he'd see Temple patiently playing baby games with Pearlie. He watched as Temp drank her pretend tea, and ate her pretend biscuits, and taught her how to catch flies with her bare hands. Bud wanted to shout to Temple, too, "Run! Why don't you run?"

It seemed that nobody needed Bud at home. The girls looked after the house. Even Temp had Pearlie to look after. But Bud had nothing and nobody. There were no cattle for him to tend, no fences to mend. There was nothing holding him there. "Run," he said to himself. "Why don't you run?"

In every childhood there's an invisible line. One day you're a boy. The next, you cross the line and you're a man. Your appearance may not change in the least, and you're unlikely to notice that anything's different at all. You mustn't expect magical transformations when crossing the line from boyhood into manhood, any more than you should expect them when crossing the 98th meridian, which marks the end of the East and the beginning of the West. You're simply in the West is all, though the difference won't be apparent till you travel quite a ways farther.

Some time after his mother died, Bud crossed that line out of childhood. In every way that anyone else could see, he was still very much a boy. But in every way that they couldn't see— that even Bud couldn't see—he was a man. He needed something to take care of, and he needed to challenge himself. And all it would take was a hint, a notion, an idea, a nudge, and he'd be out the door in search of it.

One day toward the end of the school year, Bud's daddy came home from a trip across the caprock on marshal business. He'd gone up to old Santa Fe, New Mexico, for a visit with the territorial governor in his brand-new mansion. He was fed like a king there—"Roast beef and pie, children. Nothing but roast beef and pie." Then he traveled with the governor—George Curry was his name—down through the New Mexican desert and into the lush oasis of the Pecos Valley, where, in the beautiful city of Roswell, he'd had his first taste of a fresh peach.

When Bud's daddy said the word "peach" his mouth watered so that the children could barely understand him. It was as if he had never spoken, and the children had never heard, that sweet simple word ever before. He tried to describe the sensation of fresh peach on the tongue, but words failed him. "Smell, juice, soft, sweet . . . " It was like gibberish.

The children listened with their jaws dropped, their eyes spinning with a desire to understand. Suddenly Bud was incredibly thirsty. He'd only ever eaten peaches out of cans before. Not till that moment had it even occurred to him that peaches didn't grow right there in the can.

He knew then with certainty that there was far too much he didn't know. There were too many things he hadn't seen with his own eyes or tasted with his own taste buds. That peach was Bud's last straw.

The next day, he went to Dylan and he said, "It's time. I mean it. Let's go."

"Go where?" Dylan asked.

"The caprock, Texas, New Mexico. Everywhere. The Goodnight Ranch. The Pecos Valley."

"What?" Dylan asked, stupefied. "But, Bud," he said, "my father's buying a Pierce-Arrow."

Bud just looked at him. He didn't know what he was talking about.

"A Pierce-Arrow!" Dylan said. "An automobile. A red one!"

"A stink buggy?" gasped Bud. "You'd stay here for a stink buggy?"

"Aw, Bud," said Dylan. "My mother would never let me go to the caprock. I know you're crazy, but you ain't no fool! Your father won't let you go either. You're nine, Bud. You don't even know how to multiply yet. You're *nine years old*."

"You're right," said Bud. "I'm nine. That's all I am. Just *three times three*." And he didn't—he couldn't—speak another word to anyone for the rest of the day.

★ **TEN** ★

The Ceiling

Late that night Bud lay in bed picturing in his mind the map of the West.

Slowly he pushed westward from Guthrie across the map, across the 98th meridian, across the Texas panhandle to the caprock. Once in New Mexico, he turned southward and headed down through the desert to Roswell, where he had himself a peach. From Roswell he pushed upward, to the north, up through the high desert and into the foothills of the southern Rockies to Santa Fe. Then he turned eastward, back again across the caprock. He'd just gotten to the Goodnight Ranch and was about to shake hands with Charles Goodnight himself—the one man in the world who would understand him and see his potential and perhaps even need him—and he was thinking he might stay for the rest of his life, when

45

Temple sat up beside him in bed and said in a soft whisper, "Where are you, Bud?"

Bud hadn't realized that Temp was watching him, but he wasn't startled. "I'm on the caprock. Texas, New Mexico . . . , " he said, and his voice trailed off.

"Me too," Temp sighed. He laid himself down again and folded his hands beneath his head. Then they both lay there staring at the ceiling in silence.

After a while, Temp asked, "Where's Guthrie, Bud?"

Bud pointed to a spot in the middle of the ceiling. "Right about there."

"Santy Fe?"

Bud pointed to another spot, to the left and up a bit. "There," he said.

"The peaches?"

"Down there," said Bud.

"Bud?"

"Hmmm?"

"Where's a vinegarroom?"

"Dunno," said Bud. "Could be anywhere on the caprock."

"Does a vinegarroom really have eight eyes and six legs and a terrible vinegary poison?"

"That's what Daddy says," said Bud. "It's *vinegarroon*, though, Temp."

"Is it this big?" Temp asked, stretching his arms wide apart.

"Could be," Bud said.

"Would you be scared to see one?"

"Might be. But I'd still *like* to see one."

"Me too," said Temp. "Me too, Bud. Awful bad." Temp took in several deep breaths, and then he said, "Why don't you go?"

"Go? I'm just a kid, Temp."

"No, you're not!" Temp sat up in bed and looked at Bud like he was crazy. "I'm a kid! Bud, there's *nothing* you can't do. Nothin' at all. Name one thing you can't do."

"Go to sleep, Temp," Bud said, and the words caught in his throat. Temp really was a sweet kid. "It's late."

"Remember when I could only say 'giddap' and 'glang,' Bud?"

"Yep," said Bud. "Why?"

"Just askin'," Temp said as he laid his head on the pillow again and took a deep, contented sigh.

After a while they fell asleep—four years apart but shoulder to shoulder—and together they dreamed of vinegarroons and peaches.

★ ELEVEN ★
Tumbleweeds

"Morning, Bud."

"Morning, Temp."

When the sun came up, Temp was staring right in Bud's face. He was wearing Bud's old Stetson hat—now about two sizes too big—and he was grinning. Something about the goofy way Temp was looking at him made Bud say, "Hey, Temp, why don't you spend the day with me?"

"Why not?" answered Temp, biting his lip to keep it from spreading into a ridiculous smile. "I got nothin' better to do. Feel like catching some bugs and stuff, Bud?"

"Wouldn't mind," Bud said.

They went outside, and Temp quickly caught three lizards, two grasshoppers, and several black flies. Bud had never seen anything like it before. Temp was a natural at catching stuff.

"Seems you take after Daddy," Bud said. "Don't think there's anything you couldn't catch with your bare hands."

Temp blushed from head to toe.

"How about we ride Geronimo?" Bud suggested.

"Bully!" said Temp, and he was already practically at the barn door.

They rode Geronimo together for a while—Bud behind Temp with his arms around him. After a while, Bud let Temp take the pony alone and watched in amazement as he gave Geronimo a tap and got him to gallop like a racehorse down the street. This was no easy feat, as Geronimo could be stubborn, and Temp's little legs stuck straight out from his sides so that he couldn't even properly kick him.

"Temple," Bud said, "you're a regular Comanche." Temp knew that was a compliment. The Comanches were the best horsemen on the plains. He blushed again from head to toe.

Temp wanted to ride Geronimo again and again, but finally Bud said, "Let's move on, shall we?" He got his marbles out and taught Temp how to plump from the taw line. After about an hour of that, Temp still wanted to keep going.

Bud quickly realized that Temp's philosophy of life could be summed up like this: When you find something you like to do, do it over and over again, until you're sick of doing it and everyone around you is begging you to stop. His mind was still learning simple things, but he was a smart kid and easy to get along with.

At the end of the day, when they'd run out of things to do,

they sat on the front porch, where they watched a tumbleweed roll aimlessly down the street. It must have blown in from the prairies on the outskirts of town. They followed it with their eyes, and together they sighed.

Temp said, "I think we did everything there is to do in Guthrie."

"I think so," said Bud.

The tumbleweed crashed into the neighbor's house and stopped dead. "How long will you be gone, Bud?" Temp asked.

"How long? What do you mean?"

"To Santy Fe and the place where the peaches are. And Good Morning Ranch. The *caprock*, Bud. How long?"

"Dunno," said Bud. "Could be a long time, I reckon."

"Weeks? Months?"

"Could be." Both boys got very quiet. After a while Bud turned and looked at Temp and was surprised to see that his little brow was knit into a troubled knot. "By the way, Temp," Bud said, "it's Sant*a* Fe and Good*night* Ranch."

Temp shrugged. He still had his eye on the tumbleweed. A breath of wind had gotten it rolling again. "You takin' Dylan, then?" Temp asked, his lip quivering slightly.

"Naw," said Bud. "Dylan's sweet on an automobile he ain't even met yet."

Temp perked up a bit. "You goin' alone, then, Bud?"

"S'pose so, Temp." Bud looked at his little brother hard, harder than he ever had before. Funny how he wasn't exactly a baby anymore, how he'd begun to take after their father in the face. When did that happen? And imagine learning to ride like that when he'd only been at Cross Roads a few times a year. Why, Temp could ride at least as well as Bud could at his age, and Bud was riding day and night back then.

Bud thought of Cross Roads, and he could almost hear the old mantel clock ticking. Even then, when he was Temp's age, he was ready for the caprock. He would have gone when he was five, if his mother would have let him. He would have gone alone. Bud could see now what a crazy idea that would have been. No, he wouldn't go alone. Not even now.

Bud heard two voices in his head. One was his father's: *"You must ask yourself, 'What would Mother say.'"*

The other was his mother's: *"Look after Temple. He needs you."*

That settled it. Bud was a boy of few words and quick decision. "How'd you like to come along with me, Temp?" Bud asked. "'Cause I ain't going without you."

Temp's eyes popped out of his head. "Will Daddy let us?"

Bud hadn't thought of that. "Well," he said, gulping, "there's no harm in asking. Or is there?"

★ **TWELVE** ★

Yes?

Night after night Bud and Temp locked themselves up in their room and devised their plans. They would travel across the caprock and just beyond its boundaries. They would stop mid-journey for peaches in Roswell, pass through Santa Fe for some of the governor's roast beef and pie, and save for last a visit with the great Colonel Charles Goodnight. More than anything else Bud wanted to see how he measured up against the cowboys at the Goodnight Ranch. Everything else they could leave to fate, but they simply had to make it to those three places. The longer they thought about it the more impossible it was to imagine the agony of not being allowed to go.

They knew that if they had any chance of getting their father's permission, they'd have to show him they were well-prepared. School let out for summer, but Bud was so busy he hardly even noticed. The boys studied dozens of maps and carefully worked out their route. They decided what to bring and how to divide their duties. Temp was good at lighting campfires and catching bugs, so those would be his jobs. Bud would look after everything else.

By careful calculation Bud determined that the trip should take no more than a month, and if they left by the second week of August they'd be back in time for the start of the new school year. That was September 7, the day after Labor Day. Bud didn't give a hoot about missing a day or two of school, but Temp would just be starting out this year, and he couldn't afford to miss the getting-to-know-you period.

Bud paced their room, rehearsing his speech. Temp sat draped over a chair playing the role of their father. He pretended to spit tobacco juice into a cuspidor, scratched his stomach, and picked his teeth, as their father often did. Finally, the day arrived when they could rehearse no more and they could wait no longer. August was coming fast upon them, and there was no time to waste.

"You let me do the talking, Temp," Bud said. "Best to keep things businesslike."

After supper the boys crept into the parlor, where their daddy was reading a newspaper. Bud had his maps and his notes and his diagrams tucked under his arm. His knees were shaking, and he found it difficult to speak.

Temp looked at Bud worriedly, and then he said, "Daddy," as he gave Bud a nudge.

"Yes, Temp," their daddy said, before squeezing some tobacco juice through his teeth and into the cuspidor.

Temp shot another worried glance at Bud, who was still just standing there, speechless. "Bud needs to talk to you, Daddy." Then he bit his lip.

"Yes, Bud?" said Jack, scratching his belly.

"Yes," said Bud. As he riffled through his papers and his maps, several pages fell to the floor, and he dropped to his knees to gather them up.

Temp just couldn't take it anymore. He ran to his father, jumped into his lap, looked deep into his eyes, and said in a way that would break any father's heart, "Me and Bud want to see the things you've told us about. We want *adventure*! We want to see the caprock and peaches and Santy Fe and the Goodmorning Ranch and the deadly giant vinegarroom. We want to go on a long trip, not a short one—us brothers, just us brothers. That's the important thing."

He never stopped to breathe. "Bud's got maps and plans," Temp said. "He can do anything, and he can take care of us both, because you taught him how. Didn't you go to the caprock when you were a boy? Ain't you glad you did?"

Temp blinked at his father for several seconds, while his father blinked back at him. Bud stepped forward and handed Jack the maps and the diagrams and the plans. "If we leave the second week in August," Bud said, "we'll be back in time for school."

Bud put his hand on Temp's shoulder. This was something that Temp couldn't remember him ever doing before. He blushed from head to toe.

"Please, Daddy," Bud said. "It's your fault we want it so bad."

Their father picked something out of his teeth and said, "Well, you don't expect me to say yes without thinking about it, do you?"

"No, sir," said Bud.

"No, sir," said Temp.

"We'll discuss it in the morning. Now, off to bed, the two of you."

"Yes, *sir*," they both said, sharply. Without hesitation they bolted. One by one the framed photos of Teddy Roosevelt, which hung on all the walls, fell crooked as the boys thundered past them toward their room. They threw themselves into bed without even getting undressed and spent a sleepless night gazing at the cracks in the ceiling and weighing their fate.

★ THIRTEEN ★

No?

It was a terrible night. The longest of their lives. Following a ceiling crack in one direction led Bud's mind through all the arguments against their going, at the end of which he was sure his father would say no. His heart turned to ice. But if he traced it the other way, all the reasons why they should go seemed to be as clear and as right as day, and he was sure the answer would be yes. It wasn't long, though, before he was unsure all over again.

Both boys tossed and fretted and slept not a wink. But it was all for nothing. Their father could no sooner have said no to those two desperate faces than he could have said no to himself when he was a young boy starved for adventure.

"Yes! Yes!" he said as soon as he arrived at the breakfast table the next morning. He didn't even wait to be asked.

He slammed Bud's maps onto the table, shaking the milk in Johnny's glass so that it spattered her face. "Bully!"

"What's happening?" asked Johnny in dismay, her mouth full of oatmeal. "I know something's happening!"

Temple leaped into his father's lap, threw his arms across his broad shoulders, and squeezed with all his might.

"Now, Bud," Jack said, "you've gone to an awful lot of trouble with these maps and diagrams, but haven't you forgotten two very important things?"

Bud couldn't imagine what they were. He searched his brain but came up with nothing.

His daddy grinned devilishly. "How do you plan to *get* across the caprock and all the way to Roswell and Santy Fe? By foot?"

Bud looked at him blankly.

"Well," his daddy said, "I've been thinking about it. The only way I'll let you two young boys go through that most desolate, lonely, and dangerous of places is if you, Temple, ride Geronimo. And you, Bud . . ." He paused there.

"Yes?" said Bud.

"Yes?" said Johnny. "Yes, *what?*"

"You'll just have to take Sam Bass," said their father. "You'll have to get him strong first, though. He's gathered some dust and cobwebs out there in the barn, poor fella. But he's the horse for the job. He knows his way around the caprock, all right."

Temple threw his arms around his father again and buried

his face in his chest. Temp was just past being a baby, after all, and he could get away with that sort of thing.

Bud, however, was far from a baby. His hand was trembling with excitement as he reached it toward his father for a shake. But Jack was too happy for such formalities. "Aw, come here," he said, pulling Bud onto his lap beside Temp. "You're a great boy, and I'm proud of you."

★ FOURTEEN ★

Inventory

Kitty Joe and Goldie were so angry at their father for giving the boys permission to go on such a foolhardy trip that they refused to speak to him. Johnny claimed that the reason her eyes were so red and her nose was so drippy was that she was sick with a cold, but in truth she was bitterly jealous. She was older than Temple, and more experienced, and a very good rider, but she was a girl, and that was that. She knew that she had to accept it, but she couldn't, and until the rules of the world were changed she decided to lock herself up in her room. Even if that meant forever.

As for little Pearlie, well, the idea that her brother Temple would abandon her for weeks and weeks on end—leave her high and dry—was impossible for her to believe. Temple tried to explain it to her, but she wouldn't listen.

The boys were far too busy to worry about the girls, though. First of all, they had to ride the horses hard at least twice a day if they had any chance of being ready by the second week in August.

They also had their inventory to worry about. It seemed they were always forgetting something. Every day, Bud read aloud from a list. "'Goggles, compass, wagon grease,'" said Bud. That last item was a very good salve for skin scrapes and burns.

"Check," said Temp.

"'Letter,'" read Bud.

"Check," said Temple. The letter was from their father: "To whom it may concern," it read: "These boys are Louis and Temple Abernathy. They are not runaways. Signed, their father, U.S. Marshal Jack Abernathy."

"'Checks,'" read Bud.

"Check," said Temp. Their father had opened a bank account for them with a hundred dollars in it and given them a big box of checks.

"'Whiskey,'" read Bud. In the event of a rattler bite, their father had told them, they should drink as much as they could as fast as they could, but not so much so fast that they got themselves sick.

"'Calomel,'" read Bud; it was for horsefly bites. "'Castor oil,'" read Bud; it was for just about every other ailment you could think of.

"Check. Check. Check," said Temp.

Eventually the packs were ready. Their blankets and tarps—which they called their suggans—were rolled up tight as drums. Sam's muscles were smooth and supple, his eyes were bright, and his spirits were high. He seemed to know that something was being planned for him, and he showed his pleasure in the very way he stood and breathed and faced each day. To Bud, Sam was magnificent.

The second week in August had arrived. On the morning of their departure the boys woke up at sunrise, and they were so well prepared that it took them less than twenty minutes to get ready. They slipped into their traveling clothes, strapped on their spurs, and clanked out to the barn, where they saddled and packed up the horses.

By the time Bud had given Temp a leg up onto Geronimo and gotten himself into his own seat on Sam, everyone had assembled on the porch. The girls lined up sulkily to see them off. Pearlie was the only one who looked her normal self. She still had no idea what was happening.

Bud looked like a regular cowboy in his wide-brimmed hat, his red bandanna, and his fringed gloves. Temp was a miniature version of Bud, except that his legs stuck straight out, while Bud's hung at least part of the way down Sam's sides. And Bud's old hat, which Temp insisted on wearing, was still far too big for him.

"It's a grand day to travel," said Jack, as he marched down the porch stairs and paraded like a general from Temp to Bud, inspecting their girths and stirrups. Then he spoke to Bud in such a low voice that Bud had to bend in half to hear him.

"Change of plan, son," he said.

"Sorry?" said Bud.

"You're to head from here to Cross Roads. I've talked it over with the girls, and I agree it's the best plan. It's a two-day ride. We'll take the train and meet you there. If after two days no harm has come to your brother or the horses or to you, and after riding all that way you still want to go ahead, then, all right, you'll go ahead across the caprock to Roswell, Santa Fe, and Goodnight Ranch. No one will stop you. But first you have to pass this one little test. Two days," he said. "No longer. You mustn't dawdle."

He winked at Bud, and then he raised his voice so the others could hear and he said, "Say 'so long' girls, but don't say 'good-bye,' for you'll see them again in just a couple of days."

He leaned in toward Bud and lowered his voice again. "Take the usual route, son, and don't meander or wander. Be polite to friends and strangers, and be brave boys. Rest the horses at noon. Be to bed by eight. Rise before dawn, and see us in two days." He tapped Sam's rear and said, "Glang, giddap!" and the boys were off, not to the shimmery plains or the sizzling desert or to any unknown or exotic place, but to Cross Roads, their true home, which they knew as well as they knew themselves.

★ **FIFTEEN** ★

First Steps

It was a busy day in Guthrie, and people were out in great numbers going about their business as if there were nothing more important in the world and no place they'd rather be. Bud thought that with their spurs and cowboy hats, their packs and bedrolls, he and Temple would have attracted a great deal of attention. Sam Bass, after all, was a horse well-known to be admired by Teddy Roosevelt. And yet no one even glanced at them as they rode through the streets of town. The clip-clops of the horses' hooves resounded with excitement but went unnoticed. It was as if the people of Guthrie were deaf and the boys themselves invisible.

Bud decided to take one little detour—through Snob Hill, past Dylan's house. When they got there, though, they found no one about, so Bud sighed and led Temple toward the edge of town where the dirt road would narrow to a track before disappearing altogether in the open prairie.

Just as they reached the outskirts, Bud spotted, against the pale backdrop of tall grasses and long horizons, a bright red smudge that vaguely resembled an automobile. They stopped and waited. As the vision sputtered toward them, it gained size and stature and brilliance and took Bud's breath away.

He hated to admit it, even to himself, but this was no ordinary stink buggy. It was a noble and handsome machine, suitable for a king. Therefore, Bud was greatly surprised to discover, as the automobile stopped proudly beside him, that it belonged to the Bailey family. Mr. and Mrs. Bailey sat stiffly in the front seats. Behind them sat Dylan and Maxwell. Dylan jumped up and shouted, "Bud! Look! Look! It's ours! Ain't it a beaut?"

Determined not to gawk, Bud politely tipped his hat and spurred Sam on. Temp did the same. As he sauntered past the automobile, which seemed as bright and blinding as the rising sun itself, Bud was as cool and collected as the Virginian, the cowboy hero of his favorite Western novel. As he led Temp westward toward the pale horizon, in the depths of which lay the caprock, Bud could feel the heat of Dylan's eyes on his back and knew that he was devouring the sights: the thick suggans, the saddlebags bulging with a month's provisions, the shotgun. When he heard the automobile begin to chug away, he glanced back over his shoulder and was not unpleased to see that Maxwell was thumping his head with his hand in amazement. Dylan's jaw had dropped into his lap.

"Son of a gun," Dylan mouthed as he twisted his neck to gape at the Abernathy boys as they sauntered out of town at the start of their great adventure, with spurs clanking and leather creaking. "Son of a gun!" Dylan shouted from an ever greater distance. "Son of a gun!!!"

Before the fields even came into sight, Sam seemed to sense that open land was near. He needed no urging to trot. Faster and faster he pranced, past the last little houses on the way out of town, past the cemetery where their mother was buried. The road narrowed to a rut, and then the rut disappeared, and finally they were on the open prairie.

Bud reined Sam back and stopped. "Did you remember the matches, Temp?"

"Yes, sir," Temp answered.

"Oats? Extra socks? Flour? Goggles?"

"Got 'em," Temp said.

"Well, then, I reckon we're off. Giddap!" he said, and Sam took off galloping.

"Giddap," said Temp, but Geronimo only trotted. "Glang!" he said. Temp spurred and quirted, and eventually he got Geronimo to lope. When Sam was already half a mile ahead, Temp finally persuaded his pony to gallop.

The boys whooped and hollered into the wind. The earth was a blur beneath them. Tears streamed down their faces. The horses stretched their legs and felt the full force of their strength. Sam flew over prairie dog holes and little streams and clumps of wild onion, miraculously avoiding ditch and rock and every other obstacle.

It was a struggle for Geronimo, with his short legs, to keep up. Temp didn't like being outraced, so he spurred him and quirted him. Geronimo huffed and puffed, and, just at the point where he was nosing up beside Sam, and Temple was waving and shouting, *"We caught you, we caught you,"* Geronimo got a little reckless and stepped on a snake.

This boogered him terribly. The horse reared and screeched and nearly threw Temp backward out of the saddle, but Temp held on. Geronimo whirled in his tracks. Then he bucked and kicked and hurled Temp forward onto his neck. Temp lost hold of the reins and his feet came unstirruped, but he clung to Geronimo's mane.

Geronimo took off at lightning speed across the prairie. Bud chased them, watching with horror from behind as Temp's legs flopped this way and that way over the saddle. *That's it,* Bud thought, *adventure over.*

When Geronimo lost his steam and Bud finally gained on him, Temp's shoulders were shaking violently. It looked like the poor kid was sobbing.

Bud didn't know whether to be worried or embarrassed. "Temp," he said, as he caught up, "if you're broke, we'll fix ya."

"I ain't broke!" Temp said. He wasn't crying. He was laughing so hard that he couldn't catch his breath. "A snake!" Temp had to choke out the words. "A big horse afraid of a little snake!"

"All right," said Bud, "party's over."

They trotted on, at an easy pace that cowboys call a "jiggle." Horses can trot nearly forever at a jiggle and never get tired. It's a very sensible way to travel, and the boys decided to make a habit of it.

★ SIXTEEN ★
Don't Go!

Five miles down the road they came to the house of a friend of a friend of Kitty Joe's. He seemed to be waiting for them, and insisted they stop and visit. Their father had told them to be polite, so they didn't dare refuse.

"So," the man said, "my friend tells me that your sister tells her that you boys are off to the caprock."

"Yes, sir," said Bud.

"You planning to go by the Red River?"

"Mmm-hmm," said Bud.

"You sure that's a good idea?" the man asked. "Because I knew someone once who got sucked right up in quicksand on the Red River," he said, clutching his heart. "Last thing they heard him say, as his head went under, was 'save my hat.'"

Five miles farther down the road they came to the ranch of

someone Goldie knew from school. The whole family was out on the porch, waiting for the boys, with an enormous meal laid out and two empty places at the table.

It was no easy feat for Temp to get on and off Geronimo. If when he dismounted there wasn't a porch or a tree stump for him to ease down onto, he simply had to jump. It was a long drop, and it tended to rattle the very teeth in his head. "How'd they know we were comin', Bud?" he asked before gritting his teeth and hurling himself to the ground.

"I reckon Goldie told 'em, Temp. I reckon those girls are up to somethin'."

"You boys going to the caprock? Is that right?" the father of the family asked them.

"Yes, sir," said Bud.

"What in the world do you want to go there for? Oh, Lord, they get some terrible sandstorms in that desert! Someone I used to know had their eyeballs torn right out of their sockets in a sandstorm in New Mexico. You boys want your eyeballs torn out? Why don't you just turn around and go home?"

Bud and Temp couldn't go ten miles without being pulled over by one of their sisters' friends and taken in for a meal. Everyone had a terrifying story of the caprock. Folks ambushed by outlaws hiding in caves. Struck by lightning. Lost in the desert. Stalked by wolves. Snakes in suggans. Centipedes in suggans. Almost everybody they met knew somebody who'd made the terrible mistake of drinking the water in West Texas, which was known to be poisoned with gypsum, whereupon they had suffered an excruciating illness, in many cases leading to death.

It was obvious that the girls had laid these traps for the boys. They were hoping they'd be persuaded to cancel the trip. But the boys weren't biting.

"I reckon if we get through the caprock with just half those things happening to us, we'll have a delightful journey," said Bud. "All those scary stories just make me want to go more, Temp. You?"

"Yes!" screeched Temp. "Let's goooooo."

With all the people waiting to give the boys an earful along the way, the trip to Cross Roads took two days longer than planned. Four days after leaving Guthrie, Bud spotted the stand of cottonwoods just beyond the crossroads that gave his home its name. Soon he and Temple were loping over familiar hillocks and washouts. When Bud saw Catch running toward them—his tongue flapping, his heels kicking—it seemed for a moment that things were just as they were when he was young and so happy, though he knew of course that they were not.

For one thing, there was a wild-eyed, fire-breathing, boy-eating bronco in the paddock by the house. Their father must have picked him up at an auction, but Bud couldn't imagine why. He'd never seen an angrier-looking animal. He was clearly of no use to anybody. Catch barked at the beast furiously, and pretty soon the whole family was outside, and nobody looked very happy to see the boys.

"You're two days late," said Kitty Joe.

"That's it. You can't go," said Goldie.

Their father was lurking in the shadows, hiding his face behind the brim of his hat. Bud thought he must have been sorely disappointed in them if he couldn't even look them in the eye. But then he had another thought. "Wait a minute," said Bud. "Daddy said that we should be polite to friends and strangers. Only he didn't tell us that we'd be stopped by friends nearly every ten feet." He shot accusing looks at the girls. "It's not our fault we're late, and I think you all know whose fault it is." Then he spoke to his father with a firm voice. "No one's hurt. Temp here is in one piece. And we're ready to keep going."

"Daddy," Temp said. "You promised. You wouldn't break a promise, would you?"

"No, no," their daddy said, pushing back his hat and stepping forward. "A promise is a promise. But how about we make a *deal*? A deal is a much different thing. How about you boys agree to give up your trip, if I agree to ride that mad beast in the corral there, without a saddle? I got him just for you, to give you boys a good show."

The girls were aghast. "No, thank you, Daddy," Temp said.

"What if I were to harness that untamable bronc and my nastiest bull up to that buckboard wagon over there, and see if I can get them twice around the house? Would that do it?"

"That would be a great show," said Temp, "but Bud and me have our hearts set."

"Well, I tried," said Jack. "That's all a man can do." And he
threw up his hands and walked back into the house, with the
girls moaning and complaining after him.

After two days resting up at Cross Roads, the boys were ready
to set off on their real adventure. Bud had studied his maps
and worked out their new route. Fifty miles a day, or there-
abouts, and they'd still be able to make it back to Guthrie by
September 7.

After supper, on their last night home, Johnny and Pearlie
stomped up to Bud and Temp. "You scared?" Johnny asked,
bleakly.

"Naw," Bud said. "Not really."

"Not of nothing?"

Bud shrugged. "I don't think so."

"Quicksand?"

"Nope."

"Rattlesnakes?"

"Gee, no. They're everywhere, ain't they? You ever hear of
anybody getting bit by one?"

"Gettin' lost?"

Bud shook his head no.

"Outlaws? Desperadoes? Starvation? Thirst? Insanity?"

"Guess not," Bud said.

She turned to Temple. "You?"

"Gosh no!" said Temp.

"Hmph," she said. "Well, whatever you do, don't die with your boots off. 'Cause your feet *stink*." With that she gave Pearlie's hand a tug to go, and it was then that Pearlie began to cry. Not since she was a baby had she wailed so. Temp dropped his head to his chest and felt the blood rush out of his face. He couldn't even look at her. Poor Pearlie was as lost as a tail without its donkey.

"Bud," Temp said, when she'd gone and her sobs could be heard only faintly, "bein' a big brother sure is hard." The truth was, he'd feel just the same if Bud were leaving *him* behind, and he wouldn't have traded places with Pearlie for the world.

★ SEVENTEEN ★
Go!

Jack woke the boys before dawn and dragged them down to the kitchen, where he hastily fed them porridge. "Hurry up," he said, "let's get you gone before the girls start stirring." Then he rushed them out to the barn.

As they saddled and packed the horses, he whispered to them. "You boys wire me the minute you get to Roswell. If you're not there two Tuesdays from now . . ." When he saw the way Bud's jaw dropped in disappointment, he sighed and changed his mind. "All right," he said. "By two *Wednesdays* from now, if I don't get a telegram saying you're in Roswell, I'll be on the first train to the middle of nowhere to get you and take you home.

"I don't want you dawdling and missing school," he said. "If you do get there by two Wednesdays, then I'll consider letting you make the rest of the trip to Santa Fe."

"And back across the caprock, right?" asked Bud. "To Goodnight Ranch."

"Well, we'll see," Jack said. "Don't push them horses. Rest 'em every day at noon. Don't drink the water in Texas without asking someone if it's gyppy or not. Most likely it is. Look out for quicksand, 'cause it'll gobble you right up if you're not careful. Remember everything I've ever taught you. Don't attempt to catch wolves with your bare hands. And if you meet a bad man or a bad animal that means to do you harm, don't hesitate to use this," he said, and he handed Bud a shotgun.

"It was mine when I was a boy, and it got me out of many a scrape. Keep it beside you at night when you're sleeping. And pray you won't need it. There's one bullet inside, and here's another one," he said, handing Bud a spare shotgun shell.

He walked the boys out into the dewy morning and helped them up into their seats. "Oh, to be young again," he said. "How I envy you both. Now go, git, before those girls wake up and start to nagging us all.

"Good boy, Sam," Jack said, patting his old wolf-hunting horse on the nose. "I know you'll take care of them when they can't take care of themselves. Now, off you go. Glang! Giddap!"

He slapped Sam smartly, and the boys were off, for good this time. Off they loped over the old familiar fields, as Catch ran after them, as if it were the old days—off toward the cottonwoods that sheltered the stream that marked the boundary of Cross Roads, where Bud pulled back on Sam's reins and stopped to take one last look.

Catch had halted a few yards back and was standing in the middle of the field, confused and whimpering. He'd never seen Bud cross the stream before. "Stay there, Catch," said Bud.

Bud wished he could make a picture of Cross Roads somehow, to take with him. He tried to memorize every last tree, every tuft of grass. But Sam was feeling impatient to go and would not be held back. He was already splashing through the stream, and Geronimo was following close behind. They were loping over a hill and down a gully, and Cross Roads was soon out of sight.

Everything that was familiar was behind them now. Everything ahead of them was new and uncertain.

Catch was a good dog and stayed behind, though in his heart he longed to leap into the stream and chase after them. He climbed onto a rock and watched in disbelief as the boys rode away. Long after they'd disappeared from his sight, he was still waiting there, his snout pointing westward into the wind, his whimpers traveling no more than a few feet before boomeranging into his face with the sting of dust.

When the sun grew fierce, he tucked his tail between his legs and hobbled home to wait for them in the shade, where he could hear the comforting tick-tock of the mantel clock. If he could have told time he would have known, as Johnny and little Pearlie did, that every tick was bringing the day of the boys' return nearer. But for a dog life isn't a string of weeks, days, or minutes. Until the boys came home, Catch would only watch and wait and worry.

★ EIGHTEEN ★

Time Flies

As Bud and Temple loped toward the caprock, the memory of Catch, little Pearlie, and their father seemed to evaporate like the dew on the grass. Their minds, like their bodies, moved swiftly forward, away from home. They were as free as the jackrabbits bounding across the prairie. As free as the scissor-tailed flycatchers that sliced through the air overhead. As free as the clouds floating in the pink dawn sky. Freer even than a cowboy at the Goodnight Ranch waking to the cook, crying, "Fly at it!"

Their veins tingled as if they were full of live electricity, not mere human blood. Two Wednesdays from now, their father had said. That was ages. Between now and the start of school, why, that was forever.

There were more than a thousand miles stretched, in a

meandering way, ahead of them. One thousand miles! If miles were dollars, they'd be rich. Like J.P. Morgan, the richest man in America, they didn't have to abide a lot of people telling them what to do or how to do it.

They slowed down to a trot, and Temp's little voice called from the rear: "What'll we eat for supper, Bud?" They'd only just left Cross Roads. The morning's porridge was still stuck to the roof of his mouth. "Can I have applesauce?"

"If it makes you happy," said Bud.

"Beef jerky?"

"It's a free country, Temp."

"Can't decide."

"Why not have both?"

Temp's voice quivered with pleasure. "That ain't disgustin'?"

"It is, but who's to care if *you* don't?"

"Problem solved!" Temple said, pushing his hat off his forehead and swinging one leg across the saddle in front of him, like he'd seen cowboys do when they were feeling easy and carefree. Temp's balance was not so good, though. After a teeter and a totter, he tumbled feet-over-head into the dirt.

He lay there stunned for a few seconds, during which time Bud, unaware of the mishap, carried on trotting into the wind.

Temp snapped to and hopped to his feet. "Piece o' cake," he said to himself. As it so happened, he'd fallen directly in front of a tree stump, which was just the right height to use as a mounting block. In no time at all he was back in his seat— both feet securely in stirrups—and spurring Geronimo on.

"All we have to do today," Bud said, as Temp caught him up, "is make it by nightfall to the Red River and cross it into Estelline, Texas, which is just on the other side. That should be a snap. We'll have an early supper and a good rest in a hotel in Estelline. When we wake up in the morning, we'll find ourselves well across the hundredth meridian and just a day's ride from the caprock. The *caprock*, Temp. *El llano estacado*. We're almost there."

The Estelline crossing was only sixty miles from Cross Roads. If they kept to a jiggling trot they could do six or seven miles an hour. They had more than enough time. There was no reason to kill themselves hurrying.

If Temp spotted a curious insect on a fence rail or in the dirt, Bud didn't stop him from riding over to investigate. Temp would come back with a breathless report: "I have sawn a dead swallowtail," he'd announce. Or "I think I have sawn some fly larva."

"You ain't sawn it, Temp."

"I say I did, Bud."

"You seen it, maybe, but I know you ain't sawn it."

"Oh," said Temp, and for a minute he seemed troubled with self-doubt. "But still I sawn some fly larva, right, Bud?"

They discussed matters of grammar, philosophy, geography, and superstition. Some signs, Bud said, like a red sky at night, were good luck. Others, like a dead raven on the trail, were definitely bad.

They observed strange cloud formations, unusual markings

on cattle, and the scent of wild onion crushed underfoot. Occasionally they'd make surprise attacks on prairie dog settlements and watch as the little creatures scurried about and dove headfirst into their holes, their tiny feet kicking madly behind them.

They sang the song about the famous man Sam was named after. He was an outlaw, but a good one who gave the money he stole to the poor.

> *"Sam Bass was born in Indiana,*
> *it was his native home,*
> *And at the age of seventeen*
> *young Sam began to roam."*

With all the sport and singing, Bud didn't notice the sun creeping up behind them. Suddenly, it was straight overhead. "It's noon," he observed cheerily. "Already! Why, we must have traveled close to forty miles. That means we'll be in Estelline in no time."

After a few minutes' riding they came to a ranch house, where they were given a warm welcome and invited in for the noon meal. "Climb down and eat a bean with us," the rancher said.

That's what it was like on the trail. There wasn't a homesteader or rancher anywhere in the West who would deny a traveler a meal or a bunk or a bit of advice. With so many friendly folk along the way, Bud figured getting to the caprock was going to be easy.

Until, that is, he told their host where they were headed that day. *"Estelline!?"* the rancher exclaimed. "Are you boys dumb or just foolish? Estelline is fifty miles from here!"

Bud was too polite to say so, but he thought the man must have been mistaken, not to mention rude. After all, they'd been traveling since dawn. In all that time, surely they'd traveled a good deal more than ten miles.

When they got back on the trail they kept the horses trotting smartly, but after a little while they got to feeling drowsy. Soon they were fighting losing battles against sleep. Their feet dangled from their stirrups, and their heads slumped to their chests.

As the boys drifted in and out of a most pleasant slumber, the sun dropped steadily in the west. The horses kept to the trail but carried on too slowly for the day. The afternoon crept away. The wind died down. The sky turned orange toward sunset but never softened to pink or deepened to red. The horizons pushed inward. The trail grew sandier and slower by the mile. Then night fell like a trapdoor.

That's when Temp, whose head had toppled over onto his saddle horn, was startled awake by the hoot of an owl. He jerked his head back just in time to ride into the low branch of a knobby tree, knocking the stuffing out of his head. "Stars!" he said, as his head spun. "Bud! I have sawn some stars!"

Both boys were wide awake then, in a world they didn't recognize. Hushed was the sound of the breeze through the grass. Vanished were the clouds overhead. Gone home for the night were the cattle. There was no one about but Bud, Temp, Sam, and Geronimo, with nothing but one owl and a sliver of a moon to keep them company.

And Estelline? Still untold miles away. And the quicksandy Red River, which had to be crossed that night or else they'd have no beds to sleep in, no applesauce, no beef jerky? It was surely somewhere. But how would they find it from the middle of nowhere?

"Is an owl hootin' good luck, Bud? Or is it bad luck?" Temp asked, meekly.

"I don't rightly know, Temp. But I reckon we'll soon find out."

★ NINETEEN ★

Cross a River When You Come to It

It was as dark out as a cow's insides, but there was nothing to do but carry on. And so the boys walked the horses forward, following their instincts and a shadowy trail that every few feet seemed to vanish into the night. Bud had no choice but to rely on Sam Bass not to lead them astray. Geronimo kept so close behind that his nostrils got a cleaning every time Sam twitched his tail.

It had begun to seem like they'd never find the Red River when Bud smelled something fishy and pulled back on the reins. Sam smelled it too. They both pointed their snouts into the faintest of breezes and tasted the air.

Tasted like water. Not cool fresh water, such as you swim in or drink from. It was muddy water, such as you cross at your own peril and more than likely drown in. "Smells like a boggy crossing," said Bud. "Smells like what we're after."

A couple hundred yards brought them, at last, to the bank of the Red River, just beyond which waited a cozy hotel room with a feather bed and a couple of stalls lined with fresh straw. "Better late than never," said Bud as he surveyed the bank.

All they had to do was get across. They searched through the dark for wagon tracks, but there were none to be seen, nor could they make out the other side. "We'll have to find our own way across, I reckon. You scared of quicksand, Temp?"

"Heck, no. Sam Bass ain't stupid enough to step in quicksand."

"What about, Geronimo, though? He stupid enough?"

"Heck no, he ain't stupid, Bud! He's your horse, ain't he?"

Temp may have trusted Geronimo, but Bud realized his shortcomings. For one, he could be timid. For two, he could be clumsy. "Folks say you should always cross a river when you come to it," he said. "But I just don't know."

"Why they say that, Bud?"

"I don't know, Temp. Remind me to ask someone. Don't think they had in mind the Red River on a dark night without any wagon tracks to follow. Could be quicksand out there anywhere. But I'll tell you what. Sam will know what to do. I'll walk him all the way to the water's edge and see if he fights me going in. If he pulls back, we'll camp out here and cross in the morning. You wait here till I come back for you."

Bud clucked his tongue and walked Sam slowly across the boggy bank, careful so as not to step on soft ground, which

might be quicksand. Sam sniffed the water and shook his head
in disgust. "You don't have to cross it if you don't want to, Sam,"
Bud said. "Don't reckon I'd mind at all if you didn't." Then he
gave him a light tap in the ribs and said, "Here goes nothin'."

Sam jerked back, shaking his mane hard as if he were saying
No. He quickly quieted down, though, lifted his head, swallowed some air, and without further ado plopped one hoof
into the water. It was swallowed up to the fetlock.

After just a brief disappearance, the dripping hoof
reemerged. The other ones followed quickly—so quickly that
Bud's feet were shaken loose of his stirrups. "Slow down, boy,"
he said. He lost hold of the reins, which soon were out of
reach and dangling in the water.

This wasn't the first time Sam had crossed the Red River.
That horse knew from experience stored deep in his body that
to go slowly was to court disaster. Each hoof barely even
touched the gooey bottom before it was plucked up again. As
Bud gripped his mane, Sam skimmed over the water like a
pebble. At last, the other side was in sight, and all that lay
between them and their soft clean beds was the muddy bank.

Sam charged out of the water and galloped up the incline,
and soon Bud was drenched but safe on the other side. He
flung his arms around Sam's neck and said, "Bully, Sam! That's
just about the bulliest thing I've ever seen." He grabbed the
reins, whirled Sam around, and called to the opposite bank,
"Sam did it, Temp! We're coming back for you."

"We're doin' it too!" squeaked Temp.

Bud squinted through the dark to where he'd left Temp on the other side, but Temp's voice wasn't coming from there at all. It was coming from the middle of the river. "Giddap, Geronimo!" Temp said, trying to sound stern. "Why do you want to stop here?"

There was just enough moon glow for Bud to see that Temp was in trouble. When Geronimo let out a bloodcurdling shriek that made Sam's mane shiver, there could be no mistaking it. The poor horse was up to his front knees in the river and sinking fast.

Another shriek and he was swallowed up nearly to his shoulders. His two hind legs were on firmer, higher ground, though. As he struggled to keep his head from going under, his rear end pointed to the sky like an arrow.

"Bud! We're sinkin'," cried Temp. He'd climbed out of the saddle and scooted back onto Geronimo's rump. "He wouldn't wait, Bud. He wanted to follow Sam! He wouldn't listen to me."

"Don't move, Temp," called Bud.

Geronimo's front end sank half a foot more, causing Temp to slide headfirst down the horse's back till he was clinging to its neck. "My hat, Bud!" cried Temp, clutching with one hand his beloved old oversized Stetson, now inches away from the water. "Save my hat!"

"Wait for me, Temp."

"No," said Temp. "You'll sink too. Hold your horses."

In this head-over-heels position, his mouth pressed up

against Geronimo's ear, Temp began gently to rock. "Easy does it," he whispered. "Piece o' cake," he murmured.

"Aw, Temp," Bud said. "Me and Sam are coming." He nudged Sam forward, but before they could take two steps, he heard a promising sloshing. Geronimo had started rocking too. Gently he pitched himself slightly forward and backward, loosening the sand's grip on his legs. His shrieks mellowed to gentle nickers. He and Temp carried on like that for several minutes, careful not to rush or to push too hard, lest they make matters even worse.

When he felt the moment was right, Temp cried, "Giddap, Geronimo! Glang!" Geronimo threw himself back on his rear legs, wrenched his front legs from the bog, and, with Temp scurrying back into the saddle, he pranced across the river, gingerly, as Sam had done. Then he charged up the bank to where Bud and Sam were waiting.

"What do you think of Geronimo now, Bud? Ain't he great?" Temp was breathing heavily, his eyes sparking with excitement.

Bud thought, *Imagine a kid Temp's age keeping a cool head like that. Imagine!* But what he said was "I reckon he'll do to ride the river with, Temp."

"Yes, sir, he *will*! Oh, Bud," said Temp, dripping wet. "That was an adventure, right? Please can we do it again? Please can we go back and do it again right now?"

★ **TWENTY** ★

Gypped

The hotelkeeper in Estelline didn't have any beef jerky on hand. But he had eggs and bacon, and for dessert he did have some applesauce, which he slathered on toast with brown sugar and butter. The boys had never tasted anything so delicious in their lives.

They were in bed by midnight and up by dawn, but they weren't tired at all. They were itching to move closer to the caprock. But first, on their way out of town, they decided to take a little detour past the river, just to see by daylight what they'd crossed in the starlight.

A crowd had gathered there to observe a strange scene. A farmer had been leading his mule across the river when the mule's hooves bogged in the sand. Not knowing what else to do, the mule had plopped right down in the middle of the river and had himself a sit. He'd been up to his neck in water for two hours, while the farmer tugged and tugged at him.

"Mules is stubborn beasts," said a man in the crowd.

"More like stupid," said Temp. "How does something so stupid get to be so old?"

"Dumb luck," the man said.

Bud and Temp wanted to see how the farmer got his mule out of the Red River, but they couldn't wait. It was getting late, and Bud was determined to cover the fifty miles to their next scheduled stop—Silverton—well before sundown. Time, he'd learned, was a slippery thing and you had to pay attention if you wanted to hold on to it.

"You boys look out you don't get gypped," the man in the crowd called after them, as they rode away.

They were in the part of the Texas panhandle where most of the natural water holes and streams were full of gypsum, which could make a man sick nearly to death if he drank it, and was especially dangerous for children. If they'd been warned once about it, they'd been warned a thousand times. They'd have to be pretty stupid to get gypped by bad water, after all those warnings.

"I think that's what I know best in all the world," said Temp, as they put Estelline behind them. "If I don't know 'don't get gypped,' I don't know nothin'."

It was a hot and windy day. Dust flew in their eyes and stuck between their teeth. It was an easy ride out of Estelline, though, along a well-marked trail, and they passed the time by making up private cusswords. "Granny's smelly sock," said Bud.

"Aunt Annie's fanny!" said Temp.

"Temp," Bud said. "That's a bit off-color, I'd say."

"Sorry, Bud," said Temp. "Just slipped out. I'll think of another one." As Temp worked his brain, his eyes glazed over and his horse slackened the pace.

He had fallen well behind Bud when he reached for his canteen and realized it was empty. His throat was killing him, and he was desperate for a drink. At the same time, the best parts of his brain were still at work trying to come up with good cusses. When he saw the glistening water hole just off the trail, with its edges of bright green grass, he headed straight for it.

If his brain had not been occupied reeling off cusses such as "Grandma's chin hair" and "Uncle Walt's warts," no doubt it would have stopped him from drinking the water. After all, he knew nothing better than that the water in these parts was poison.

But there it was, this water hole, and beside it a tree stump, just the right height for Temp to hop onto without having to stop his train of thought. "Bert's burp." "Old Pa's poo." That one cracked him up. He flopped on his belly and kicked up his heels as he filled his canteen to the brim. Then he hopped onto the stump and into his seat. He was back on the trail in no time and raising the canteen to his lips.

He'd gulped down almost half of the water before something in his mouth alerted his brain. "Aunt Annie's fanny!" he griped. "Tastes disgustin'!"

At that same moment, Bud was turning around to say, "Shame all this water is gyppy. I'm plum out, and I'm parched."

The wheels of Temp's brain then ground to a halt and began spinning in the opposite direction. He dropped his reins, clutched his throat with both hands, and began forcibly to gag.

"What's got you?" Bud asked. "You look buggy."

"I'm a goner," said Temp. Geronimo's ears swiveled in alarm. "I been gypped, Bud. I'm a dumb mule. You just leave me here. You keep goin' without me. I'm a goner for keeps."

★ TWENTY-ONE ★
Goner

Temp griped all the way to the town of Turkey, where Bud decided they ought to stop and stay the night in a hotel. "Far as I can see," he said, "you ain't sick yet, Temp, and you might never get sick. But let's stay here and see what happens. We're still twenty miles from Silverton, but we can make the distance up tomorrow."

"If I don't die, you mean. Right, Bud?"

"If you're dead, we ain't goin'. That's final."

At suppertime Temp still was feeling fine enough to gobble down a big plate of franks and beans. But ten minutes later his face turned green and he made haste for the privy, where he remained for the rest of the night.

"My stomach's a volcano," Temp groaned through the door. "My head feels like my throat's been cut open. I'm a goner for

keeps." Eventually he fell asleep in the privy. Bud slept on the
ground outside, thinking the trip was doomed and he never
should have taken Temp along.

*He's just a baby, after all, and he needs someone better taking
care of him,* Bud thought. *Daddy never would have let a thing
like this happen.*

"It's my fault, Bud," Temp said the next morning. "I'm the
dumb mule."

"I should've been watching you, Temp. It's my fault."

"No, Bud. It's *mine.*"

"No, Temp. It's mine."

"It's mine, Bud."

"It's *yours*, Temp."

"It's *yours*, Bud."

"That's what I said. Now let's go find you a doctor, and
then let's go home." Sorry as he was that Temp was deathly
sick, he had to admit to himself that his own disappointment
was an even sharper pain in his heart. *Goodnight, Charles
Goodnight,* he thought to himself, as he gazed with melan-
choly in the general direction of the caprock.

"What!?" exclaimed Temp. "Home? Doctor? Why, I ain't
dead, am I, Bud? I'm a *little* sick is all. I'll be fine. C'mon, Bud.
I want to go to Silverton now. Let's get the horses and go."

Bud was encouraged by Temp's pep. *Good morning, Colonel
Goodnight!* But before he could decide what to do, he wanted to
see how Temp did with breakfast. He took him into the hotel
and watched him eat some eggs and sip some water. When he

saw that it went down all right and didn't come out the other end right away, he determined that maybe it was all right to carry on.

"We'll go," said Bud. "But you've got to take some medicine." He dug around in his saddlebag and plucked out a bottle of castor oil. "Here we go. Just the thing. Cures everything." He made Temp take a big dose of it.

"Tastes like vomit!" said Temp.

"That's 'cause it's good for you," said Bud. "It'll fix you right up. Don't know why I didn't think to give you any last night. Now, let's go. If we ride ten extra miles every day for three days, we'll make up the time we lost yesterday. And we'll be right back on schedule and rolling into Roswell two Wednesdays from now."

They headed out of town with the highest of hopes. For a few miles everything went smooth as silk. The boys sang a verse of the Sam Bass song, and Temp's voice wavered only slightly. A short while later, though, Bud realized he hadn't heard a peep out of Temp for several minutes, so he turned around to check on him.

Temp was nowhere. He'd vanished. Geronimo was off the trail, sniffing for grass. His saddle was empty, his reins were dangling, and his stirrups were swinging.

Bud frantically scanned the area until finally he spotted Temp's head poking up from behind a dwarf mesquite tree that he appeared to be squatting behind. Bud watched in bewilderment as his brother untied his red bandanna from around his neck. "What are you up to there?" asked Bud.

Temp's face turned as red as the bandanna. "Using it to wipe my bottom," he shouted crossly. "Don't look, Bud."

"Why shouldn't I? I can't see nothin' anyway."

"Just don't." When he was sure Bud wasn't looking, Temp finished wiping himself. Then he stood up, pulled up his pants, and, not knowing what else to do with it, he carefully folded the bandanna into a neat little square and shoved it into his back pocket. "Now you can look," he said, "but please don't say nothin' Bud."

Without saying a word, Bud made him take a few more swigs of castor oil and helped him back up into his saddle. "That stuff is what's making me sick," said Temp.

"Don't be crazy," said Bud. "It's medicine. Medicine can't make you sick."

"I said don't say nothin'."

"Sorry, Temp," said Bud. "Oops. Now I've done it again. Sorry."

"*Please* stop talkin', Bud."

It was less than twenty miles to the next town, called Quitaque, but it might as well have been a hundred. Whenever Bud turned around to check on Temp, he would find him scampering about, waving his bandanna, looking for a place to relieve his misery, while Geronimo munched away on grass completely unconcerned.

To make matters worse, all the climbing up and jumping

out of the saddle had caused both of Temp's ankles to swell up like giant raw sausages inside his boots. Every scamper was a new kind of misery.

By the time they got to Quitaque the bottle of castor oil was empty. And Temp was an empty bottle too. His head drooped to his belly, and he rode into town like a dead man on a dying horse.

"I'll go to the general store and get you some other medicine," Bud said.

"No," said Temp, sounding drunk. "*I'll* go. If *you* go, you'll just get more of *that*," he said, pointing a withering finger at the saddlebag that held the vile oil.

Just as Temple was preparing himself to jump from the saddle onto his aching feet, Geronimo was overcome by a new sort of feeling of mercy. He surprised Temp by snorting kindly and stretching out his front left leg. "Thank you, Geronimo. I'm much obliged," said Temp, as he slid down the out-stretched leg and limped inside the general store.

"Castor oil!" exclaimed the lady behind the counter. "For gyp poisoning?! Heavens no. That's the *worst* thing for it."

Temp glared at Bud, whose heart sank to his spurs.

"You poor child," the lady said, as she rushed to Temp, took him in her lap and pried off his boots. "You look like you've had a month of troubles."

"Two days," groaned Temp.

She slathered his ankles with plasters. She spooned soft little sips of milk into his mouth and fed him tiny morsels of bread. Then she gave him a dose of Vin Vitae and a lollipop, and he was soon his old self again. The boys carried on traveling, but they spoke not a word for hours.

When at last they arrived at Silverton, Geronimo stretched his leg forward again and Temp slid down it like a prince. He didn't seem at all surprised when at the livery stable a man started shouting, "It's them boys! It's them boys what we heard was coming! Them Abernathy boys!"

To Bud, though, it came as a real amazement to discover that a bit of fame had preceded them to town. Word of mouth had spread from Estelline to Turkey to Quitaque and now to Silverton. Soon dozens of folk had rushed out of their homes and their shops to see the nearly famous boys from Oklahoma—one, so stupid that he gypped himself; the other, a boy who'd nearly killed his own brother with castor oil.

A teenage boy burst from the hotel with a cornet and played "There'll Be a Hot Time in the Old Town Tonight." Someone turned over two wooden crates and lifted each boy onto one. Speeches were made and praises were sung. No one had ever seen two little boys so far away from home.

The people gathered there were stunned and amazed by all they had heard of the boys' journey so far. But they weren't nearly as shocked as they were to learn that they were headed next into the farthest place from anyone's idea of home—a place that made grown men go mad: *El llano estacado.* The staked plains. *The caprock.*

★ TWENTY-TWO ★
Insanity

In the dark of the morning, as they rode out of Silverton, the boy with the cornet called to them, "You boys hold on to your senses. There's a whole lot of nothin' out there on that caprock, and it can play tricks on your mind." Then he serenaded them with "Goodbye Dolly Gray," as a few shopkeepers came out to sing along:

> *"Don't you hear the tramp of feet, Dolly Gray,*
> *Sounding through the village street, Dolly Gray."*

Fifteen minutes later, when Bud turned to look behind him, he saw no trace of the town and could no longer hear any whisper of civilization. All that he could see was a vast plain that reached all the way to what people in those parts called a "prairie aurora": the rays of the rising sun fanned across the eastern sky like the spokes of a wheel.

Ahead, though! Ahead of them, to the west, and beside them, to the north, appeared the outlines of fantastic shapes that were difficult to believe. Mammoth rocks shaped like spires and arches, castles with turrets, gigantic lighthouses, and sky-scraping ladders loomed above the plains.

This was it, Bud realized. They were inching up to the caprock. "Temp," he said, pointing beyond the northern horizon. "Look. Way over there is the famous Palo Duro Canyon. The 'Grand Canyon' of Texas. And the Goodnight Ranch is just on the other side."

But Temp was already asleep in the saddle, and he had none too sure a grip on it. His ankles were still so swollen that he'd only managed to stuff a few toes into the feet of his boots, which now were wedged into his stirrups half empty. Bud was afraid to wake him, lest he startle and fall off again. He let him sleep and took in the sights alone.

By the time Temp woke up, the fantastic shapes were behind them. The land all around them was flat and brown. It was as if all of that strangeness had sunk back down into the earth's center. It was as if it had all been a trick. "Tricks, already," said Bud. "I ain't letting it drive me mad, Sam. I just ain't."

"You talking to yourself, Bud?"

"It's the caprock, Temp," Bud said. "We're here. This is the loneliest, most desolate, flattest, most vast and wonderful place in the world."

They were in a land that seemed as unlike their native habitat as they imagined the sea was. The choppy short grass was like waves. The windmills that occasionally popped up on the horizon were like the masts of ships. Like the sea, there seemed to be no end to the caprock and no beginning. It was just as their father had said.

Before he got used to it, Bud felt a little seasick. "Why's your skin green?" Temp asked, slyly. "Better have some castor oil, Bud. Better have it quick."

"Please don't say nothin'," said Bud with a burp, as Temple snickered.

Every horizon seemed to stretch on to the edge of infinity, whereupon it melted and oozed over the rim. There was nothing of life but tumbleweeds, scurrying tarantulas, a few stunted mesquite trees, a cactus here and there, and the occasional windmill.

And there was the wind. Strong and steady, it never gusted or twirled. It didn't change direction on a whim. It wasn't sneaky. As they pressed into it, the wind filled them up and made them feel twice their real size.

For sport, they counted windmills. The deeper they traveled into the caprock, the greater the number and variety of them. Some, they noted, had one wheel, while others had two. Some had vanes, some were vaneless. Some opened and closed like an umbrella gulping up the wind, but most just spun and spun and never stopped. Their favorites were the ones marked "Original Star," which were painted red, white, and blue.

During the next few days, they passed through some small towns, but they chose to sleep out-of-doors, beneath the stars, where the nights were cool. Temp would make a fire, while Bud laid their horsehair rope on the ground, in a circle around their camp, to keep out snakes and centipedes.

By dawn the heat was already on the rise. The cool water they filled their canteens with each morning was hot by ten A.M. After a while, they lost track of the date and went for a long time without seeing another human soul. Their heads swam, and they began to wonder if perhaps the caprock was driving them insane.

They saw mirages. At first the visions were just of flat pools of water that spread across the horizon and seemed to evaporate as the boys got near. After a while, though, the mirages took on far more complicated shapes. Indian war parties materialized out of thin air. A long line of prairie schooners—covered wagons such as the early settlers used to travel westward across the country—slithered along the horizon. A real herd of cattle looked from the distance like a forest. And then it became a graveyard. And then it turned upside down and became a herd of cattle standing on their heads.

At first they tried to ignore these visions. But after a while they gave in and decided they themselves might as well be mirages too. They pretended they were pirates at sea. Then they were Comanches and took turns being Quanah Parker, the famous warrior and chief. They pretended to be conquistadors, explorers from Spain, in search of Quivira, the city of gold.

When they saw the mirage of an Indian war party, they became buffalo soldiers and engaged them in battle. When it appeared that a waterfall was tumbling onto the caprock from a peach-shaped cloud, they dove right into it and splashed around till they convinced themselves they were drenched. They vowed they'd never tell a soul about the things they believed. That would be embarrassing. But it didn't stop them believing.

"I reckon we're crazy, Temp," said Bud, as he rode toward a mirage of a train station, complete with a Harvey House restaurant and a dozen Harvey Girls all lined up and waving at them.

"I reckon so, Bud," said Temp, with visions of strawberry sodas and thick, juicy steaks before his eyes. "But I don't mind at all. Do you? It sure beats nothin', don't it Bud?"

★ TWENTY-THREE ★

Ace

One day near noon, when the sun was highest and their brains were baking, they saw the strangest mirage of all. It looked like a two-headed dragon, with a white bulbous body and a black tail that coiled around itself. It breathed fire, too, but not from the mouth. This dragon breathed its fire from its other end.

As they got closer, it refused to vanish. Nor did it creep back as they crept forward, which was what most mirages did. This one just kept getting bigger and bigger and bigger. "Should we go around it, Bud?" Temp asked in a thin voice. He didn't like the looks of this dragon.

But Bud was feeling conquistadorial, and he said, "I'm not going to be scared away by a mirage. If it's a fire-breathing dragon, I reckon we'll have to slay it. Giddap, Sam!" he commanded, and Sam, who was hungry for adventure and only too willing to obey, galloped across the plain.

"Giddap, Geronimo!" said Temp. After another "giddap" or two, a few smacks of the quirt, and one "pretty please," Geronimo galloped full tilt toward the dragon.

It wasn't till they were practically right on top of it that they saw that it was only a double-headed windmill, at the foot of which sat a covered wagon and a sad old nag and a campfire.

"Yoo-hoo, you boys," they heard. Where the voice came from, they couldn't say. It hadn't come from inside the wagon. It hadn't come from the old nag. "Up here," the voice cried. "*Way* up!"

They lifted their chins as high as they could, and at last they saw a speck of a man. He was standing on the tip of the windmill vane, with nothing holding him up but his suspenders. The wind blew his hat off, but he was as sturdy on his spot as Bud and Temp were on theirs. "I said to myself," he called, "'Two little boys out alone on the caprock? Impossible! Must be a mirage!'"

He shimmied like a monkey down the rungs of the windmill tower. "Asa Conover," he said, as he plopped to the ground and reached to shake their hands. "But you can call me Ace. Everybody else around here does. I'm a windmiller. This whole territory is mine. I go 'round and 'round and 'round to all of the windmills and fix them up when they're broke."

He was a small fellow dressed in overalls. He had sandy hair and a boyish way of moving about. From a distance he looked not much older than Bud. Up close, though, they could see that he had quite a few wrinkles on his face, mostly around his eyes. Bud and Temp weren't sure at all about his age. He acted like a twelve-year-old. But he might have been as old as, say, thirty.

"Whoa," Ace said in excitement, as his eyes shot for something that was poking out of the dirt. "What is *that*?" He took three bounding leaps, fell to his knees, and dug it out. "Just what I thought," he said. "Arrowhead. Comanche, I reckon."

He showed it to Temp. "What do you think?"

"Could be Comanche," Temp said.

"I ought to send it to the Smithsonian Institute," Ace said. "But I like it so much, I don't think I can part with it."

He filled up their canteens with water from the windmill tank and invited the boys to have some slumgullion stew. After lunch, Temp crawled around looking for giant vinegarroons while Bud lay on his back, gazing at the sky and chatting with Ace. Bud was glad for a bit of adult conversation.

"If it's not rude to ask," Ace said, "what are you boys doing out here, anyway?"

Bud explained how they were on a trip to Santa Fe, by way of the caprock and the Pecos Valley, and then home again by way of the Goodnight Ranch.

"That's peculiar," Ace said. "Maybe I should send *you* to the Smithsonian Institute."

Bud laughed and lifted his head off the ground, and just then he had the most disturbing sensation. The land was so flat and featureless that he could see nothing—absolutely nothing—beyond his feet. It was as if the world had shrunk down precisely to the size of Bud.

"So have you found anything worth keeping?" Ace asked. "Any souvenirs? Any dofunnies?"

"Ain't seen nothing but tumbleweed and tarantulas."

"We'd like to see a giant vinegarroom," Temp shouted from afar, his voice faint and distant. "Can you show us one?"

"I don't see many of those awful monsters," Ace said. "Thank goodness. And if I do I keep my eyes shut. Most of what I see is rattlers. There's probably a whole army of them right inside here," he said, patting a little door into the windmill's wooden base, which held the works and the pump.

"Shall we see?" he asked.

"Why not?" said Bud, sitting up. His head spun in a pleasant way.

Ace grabbed a long stick out of his wagon. Then he opened the little door and poked his body inside up to his waist. When he came out again he had a rattler dangling at the end of the stick, which, with a smart flick, he flung halfway across the caprock. He plucked out rattler after rattler and flung them farther than Bud's eye could see. They'd catch the breeze just so and, gently spinning, would seem to float over the earth.

"They travel far when the wind's right," Ace said. "Good wind like this at your back, you can fling a rattler to the ends of the earth. Don't want it much stronger than this, though.

I've seen houses plucked up in a fierce wind. Trees uprooted. Men slung like arrows. But one thing I've never seen is a horse that couldn't stand up even to the most furious wind. Why's that?" Ace asked Bud.

"Dunno," Bud said. "Wish I did."

"Ain't she a beauty?" said Ace, rubbing his old nag between her ears. "She's my very best friend." She was rigged up now and ready to go. "Well, Bud," Ace said, "I'm afraid I have to say adios."

Bud hated to see him go. "Couldn't you travel with us a bit?"

"Sorry, but I don't do New Mexico. Toooo many sheep in New Mexico." He screwed up his face and said with disgust, "Sheep stink."

"Couldn't you just come a mile or two?"

"But, Bud," Ace said. "Ten more steps *that*away and you'll be there, in New Mexico."

"Is that right?" asked Bud, gazing thataway.

"It bothers me, though," said Ace, "that you boys don't have anything to bring home for your mother. Seems bad manners."

"That's all right," Bud said. "Our mother's dead. She don't need nothing."

Asa was taken aback by this information. "Oh, so it's just you and your brother and these two horses, then? I didn't know." He looked very sad. Tears filled his eyes, but before they could tumble out he thought of something to cheer himself up. "Wait!" he said. "I've got just the thing. Come with me into my tepee."

He led Bud into his wagon, where in every corner there were piles of rusty tools and canned food and bedraggled bedding and dozens of tins that were full of things like arrowheads, snake skeletons, bits of ancient pottery, and scraps of armor he said had belonged to conquistadors.

"When it pops into my head to give something to someone, then I don't think twice. I give it to them, no matter how much it hurts. That's my philosophy," said Ace, as he reached into a tin and pulled out a strand of beads with a little leather pouch dangling at the end. "This," he said, "is a Comanche medicine charm. Sewn up inside this little pouch is a real umbilical cord. A Comanche fella told me so himself. It's meant to connect a child to his mother forever, even if she's dead." He looked at Bud with an expression of total glee. "Well?" he said. "Isn't it just perfect?"

"Yes, it is," said Bud, politely. "Thank you, Ace."

"You be careful out there, son," said Ace. He put a fatherly arm around him. "Don't be afraid. And whatever you do, don't climb any windmills. It's much more dangerous than I make it look. Anyway, you ain't missin' nothin'. The caprock looks just the same up there as it does down here."

★ TWENTY-FOUR ★
Desperadoes

If Asa was right and they really were about to cross into New Mexico, then civilization was only twenty miles away. The town of Portales was a major stop on the Santa Fe line, and it looked on Bud's map to be plenty big enough to have stores and a hotel and maybe even someone who could tell him the meaning of *ulbimical.* Or was it *umblimcal?*

"I ain't seen *one* vinegarroom!" Temp complained as Bud helped him up on Geronimo.

"It's vinegarroon, Temp."

"That's what I said, ain't it?" snapped Temp.

Bud looked at Temp funny. "What's different about you? Have you changed? You look . . . well, you look *mean.*"

"It ain't much farther to New Mexico, is it, Bud?" Temp's voice was strangely hard and humorless.

Bud got on Sam, gave him a little kick, and said, "I'm glad you asked." He counted Sam's steps—onetwothreefourfivesix-seveneightnine . . . *ten*! "Here it is, Temp. New Mexico. That fast enough for you?"

"That was *good*," Temp said, cheering up. But after looking around a bit, his face drooped again. "Looks just like Texas."

The boys were hot, tired, and dirty. They had dust in their eyes, their teeth, between their toes, and even in their under-pants. The skin on their inside thighs had been rubbed as raw as steak. Their throats were parched. They were sick and tired of drinking their cold water warm. They'd become a bit irritable.

"Maybe the people in Portales have heard about us," Bud said. "Maybe there'll be a big party, like there was in Silverton. We'll stay overnight in a nice hotel with a feather bed and a porcelain bathtub. Then from there all we have to do is follow the train tracks to Roswell. Now, I'm not sure if today's Sunday or if it's Monday. But I reckon if we travel smart we won't have any trouble getting to Roswell by Wednesday."

Temp seemed cheered up again. Ten peaceful minutes passed before Temp said, "We almost in Portales, Bud?"

"No, we are not," Bud answered. "I said twenty miles."

"Just askin'," Temp said.

About ten minutes later, Temp asked, "When will we be *almost* there, Bud?"

"Ask me again in three hours, Temp."

Again they rode in silence until, after a short while, Temp's little voice squeaked, "Bud?"

"No, we're not almost there."

"I *know*," said Temp. "I wasn't going to ask that."

"What, then?"

"Um," said Temp. "Nothin'."

Twenty miles with Temp's infernal questioning felt like twenty days. When at last they staggered into town they were two mean, grimy boys on two filthy, fed-up horses. They hitched up in front of the post office and looked about, thinking there'd better be something good in this town, and it better happen fast. *There had better be cornets.*

At last, a man came running out of the post office and excitedly said, "Hey there, you boys!"

Bud turned to him, prepared to say, "Yes, it's us. Louis and Temple, the boys you heard about. What took you so long?"

But the man had a pinched and angry look on his face. "Go. Git," he said. The boys blinked at him numbly. "You heard me," the man said. "You boys can't leave them filthy horses there. Go on. Git."

In the general store across the street, the clerk watched them suspiciously as they browsed among his goods. Temp spotted a nice bandanna, something he sorely needed, but before he could ask for a price he was given a shock. "Take your hands off that glass countertop, boy," the clerk snapped, as he smacked Temp's hand with his grab stick.

"Ouch!" cried Temp.

"Both of you git out of here. Go on, git."

Outside they took a good look at each other. Neither one

of them had bathed in well over a week. They smelled foul, a bit like dogs that have been rolling in manure in a rain shower. But Bud didn't think they looked *that* bad. Temp's little baby face was far from sinister.

"Do I look like an outlaw?" Bud asked.

"Yep, you do," said Temp. "Do I? Do I look like that fellow, A.Z.Y.? The one with all the white teeth on the poster in Daddy's office?" He flashed Bud a wide, phony smile.

"Much meaner. I reckon if Billy the Kid saw you right now he'd go running to his mommy. What say we give the folks at the hotel a fright?"

They clanged in their spurs up the steps to the hotel. Bud reached for the door and opened it, creakingly. Just as he was lifting his foot over the threshold, an inhospitable voice from within hissed, "Oh no you don't, you devils. Git. Shoo."

Bud and Temp looked at each other, shrugged, and walked over to the horses. "I reckon we ain't welcome in this town, Temp," said Bud. "What say we head on out?"

"Yes, sir, compadre."

They would have flown out of Portales that instant, if only they didn't really need to get some things from that general store. Without them, they'd starve. Bud was just going to have to go back in there. "Here goes nothin'," he said. He took a deep breath, rummaged for something in his saddlebag, and ambled back toward the store, saying, "I hoped I wouldn't need this."

He stood in the open doorway like a desperado from the

olden days. From his hip, he raised his box of bank checks, aiming them at the clerk, like a six-shooter. "Me and my brother need food and water," he said firmly. I mean business. Help us now, and we won't trouble you again."

The clerk grunted unhappily, but he did as he was told, reaching with his grab stick for the things Bud ordered and tossing them into a sack. "Throw a nice red bandanna in there, too, while you're at it," Bud said. "Not that small one that looks pink and sickly. Give us that nice big bright red one." His heart was pounding, but his check-box hand was steady.

Afterward, as the boys followed the train tracks out of Portales, they carried with them the not unpleasant feeling of being outcasts and outlaws. It bound them together and made them feel kindly toward all creatures who had ever been misunderstood and banished to the hard places of the world.

It wasn't long, though, before they felt like two little lonely boys again. When they saw that night was falling fast and got a good look at the desolate New Mexican desert into which they'd been exiled, they longed for the hospitality, meager as it was, back in Portales.

★ TWENTY-FIVE ★
'Rooned

When the boys spotted what looked like the outlines of a house—about a mile west from where they stood near the train tracks—they figured it for a mirage. But their hopes were much greater than their doubts, and they left the trail and headed for it.

What they found was just a little abandoned one-room house made of adobe. Half the back wall had rotted away and the roof was caved in, but it was real and it would do. "Well, Temp," said Bud. "I reckon it's ours if we want it. Looks like a good hideout."

While the horses rolled on their backs, Temp gathered some firewood. Bud went into the house with a stick to poke around for snakes and came out dangling a big rattler with a chattering tail. He held it at arm's length. "What ya gonna do with it, Bud?" Temp asked.

"Dunno. I could shoot it, or mash it with a rock. I could stomp on its head with the heel of my boot. Or I could take it by the tail and snap it like a whip, which would break its spine. Or I suppose I could fling it. Not a very good wind for flinging tonight, though."

It seemed to Bud that rattlers were among the most misunderstood of any of the creatures of the world. Every other animal despised them—especially, it seemed, the ones who had the least to fear from them. If ever there was a compadre to the desperadoes of the world, it was the rattler. Bud carried him about fifty paces away and left him safely behind a cactus.

After supper the boys hobbled the horses near the gap in the wall, where they could see them, and spread out their suggans in the most protected corner of the little house. Bud circled their beds with the horsehair rope, and both boys wrapped themselves tight in their blankets. The shotgun lay within reach of Bud's right hand.

The world dimmed, and soon it was very dark. Their eyes fluttered shut, and blackness filled their heads. Meanwhile, the desert around them came to life. The centipedes, Gila monsters, horned toads, and all the lizards that were too clever to come out during the day, when the sun could kill you, came creeping out now from their holes and their burrows. As the morning neared, they were still nosing around in search of food, many of them in places where they didn't belong—the nests and burrows of animals and boys who were trying to sleep.

Just before dawn, Temp screamed, "Bud!"

"What is it?" Bud cried. "What?"

"Somebody's in my suggans with me."

"Rattler?" asked Bud, gripping his shotgun and training it on Temp.

"Wait! Don't shoot. Peel me, Bud. Go on."

"If you say so," Bud said. He peeled back Temp's blankets, one after the other, after the other.

"Well?" asked Temp, now fully exposed, his eyes squeezed tight.

"Diabalo!" Bud exclaimed.

"What is it?"

There on Temp's stomach, slicing the air with his deadly sharp pincers, whipping his tail over his head, and staring daggers into Temp with all eight of his googly eyes, was a beast that could only be the famed giant vinegarroon. There could be no mistake about what he was. The question was, what did the killer *want*?

Temp opened his eyes and beheld him. "Diabalo," he gasped. Then, slowly, his right hand crept along the blankets toward the creature.

"Stop!" cried Bud. "Have you gone insane?" But it was too late. The beast whipped its tail madly overhead and squirted Temp's fingers with his venom. The smell of vinegar filled the air.

"*Aaaaaugh!*" screamed Temp.

"*Aaaaaugh!*" screamed Bud.

Sam whinnied, and Geronimo yanked his hobbles.

With a pounding heart, Bud dove for his pack and rummaged around for the bottle of whiskey. "Aw, no," he said to himself. "That's for rattler bites." Desperate to do something, he grabbed the castor oil and rushed back with it to Temp.

"*Stop—right—there,*" commanded Temp. The mere sight of the bottle made his stomach do flip-flops. "It burned a little at first. But now it don't hurt at all. Don't go killin' me, Bud!"

The giant vinegarroon was thrashing amid the hills and valleys of Temp's crumpled blankets, groping his way around like a blind man. He was no more than half a foot long from head to tip of tail. "Ain't much of a giant. I think I can take him alone," said Temp.

Slowly he inched his hand again along the blankets. Carefully he placed one finger on either side of the 'roon's hard body. Delicately he lifted him into the air and within three inches of his nose, from which distance he examined him. Temp plopped him into the open palm of his other hand, and then, heedless of the danger, he caressed him. He petted him, like a puppy dog.

"You sure that's smart?" asked Bud.

"He's ugly," said Temp. "But he's cute."

The little 'roon seemed completely tame now. His pincers were folded demurely on Temp's hand. His tail wasn't whipping so much as it was wagging. "Oh, Bud," Temp said. "Thank you for taking me here. Thank you for bringing me to the caprock. You're the best big brother there ever was. This is the best day of my life. Thank you, Bud. Please, Bud, can I keep him?"

★ TWENTY-SIX ★
Brotherhood of United Travelers

The traveling party had grown by one. "Vinegarrooms is *nocturnal*, Bud," said Temp. "They can't stand the sun." Before they headed out again, he'd put the 'roon in an empty tin can, which he covered with a piece of burlap and stowed in his saddlebag, where at least it was shady.

"Neither can I," said Bud, as they rode in search of the train tracks they'd left the night before. The sun was scorching. "Where'd you learn that word, *nocturnal*, Temp?"

"Dunno," he said, sighing. "Sometimes words just come to me." His eyes were bloodshot and his lids were limp.

It was no day to be out if you were a vinegarroon or a pale-skinned boy or a horse, either. By noon their saddles smelled like burning leather, and the boys themselves were suffocating. Sam and Geronimo were dragging their hooves like a couple of old nags, and the tracks were still nowhere in sight.

"How could I lose those train tracks?" said Bud. As he surveyed the desert, the sun burned him right through his clothes and cooked his brain. He raised his canteen to his cracked lips and sucked in water so hot that it scalded his tongue. It was undrinkable.

"Temp?" Bud said. "You alive?" Temp's head was slumped to his chest. He looked as withered as a dead weed.

Temp shook his head, *no*. "We're goners for keeps," he said, listlessly.

"Dang it," said Bud. He tugged on the reins and jumped to the ground, where he scouted about for a handful of pebbles. "Suck on these," he said, as he handed Temp two of the pebbles and plopped another two onto his own parched tongue. "It'll play a trick on your brain. Make you think you're not thirsty."

As they rolled their pebbles around in their mouths and took in the emptiness that surrounded them, Temp's eyes got as big as saucers.

"What happened? You swallow one?" asked Bud.

Temp shook his head, *no*. "My brain's playing tricks on me," he croaked, and pointed out into the middle of the desert, where a puff of dust was stirring up a fuss and seemed to be headed their way. "Is it a tornado, Bud?"

"I don't know *what* it is, Temp." But, plain as day, Bud saw it too.

"Dust devil?"

"Let's not wait to find out. Let's jingle our spurs. Let's high-tail it." He jumped on Sam, spurred him, quirted him, but the horses were both sun-drunk and they weren't going anywhere fast. Meanwhile, the tornado was practically upon them. And it was calling them. "Boys!" it was saying. "Yoo-hoo, you boys!!!"

They rubbed their eyes and watched as from the cloud of dust there emerged a horse-driven buggy in which there sat a cool, shiny vision of a man. He had a straw hat perched high on his head and wore a crisp linen jacket with striped white trousers. There wasn't a bead of sweat or a wrinkle or a speck of dust to be seen anywhere on him. Beside him on the bench, like first-class passengers, sat two leather cases. Affixed to one was a brass tag engraved with the word "Hardware." On the other was a tag etched with the word "Software."

He pulled his horse to a halt and grinned broadly at the boys and then he started laughing. Bud and Temp were dumbfounded and couldn't even speak as they took in the spiffy suit, the polished shoes, the leather cases, and the look of confidence about this man. His tinkling laughter filled their heads and made them feel like they were floating.

"Wait a minute," Bud said. "You're a drummer, ain't you?"

"Now, now," the man said. "No need for insults. My father was a drummer, but I'm a man of *modern* commerce." As way of proof, he showed Bud a pin on his lapel. "You'll recognize this, no doubt, as the grip and crescent, emblem of the Order of United Commercial Travelers, of which I'm a registered member." He offered his hand for Bud to shake. "Name's Richard Hunt, traveling salesman. Pleased to meet you."

He took Bud's hot, sweaty hand in his to shake it, and when he felt its shriveled lifelessness, he said despairingly, "Oh my. You boys are in a terrible way." From under his seat he plucked two canteens, each one wrapped in cool wet burlap. "Go on, don't be shy," he said to the boys. "Mother Nature's supply is infinite. Splash some on your faces too. Go on," he said. The boys gulped the water down eagerly. It was the sweetest, coolest taste they'd ever known.

When they'd drained the canteens dry, the drummer led them to a desert oasis—a clean, clear water hole surrounded by lush green grass—that seemed to appear out of nowhere, like a mirage. "This is my territory," he said, with a sweep of his hand across the empty horizon. "I know it as I know my own mind."

The boys filled their canteens and wrapped them in wet burlap. Then they flopped on their stomachs beside the horses and drank till their stomachs ached.

When they were feeling better, Bud said, "Mr. Hunt?"

"My father was Mr. Hunt, Bud. Call me Dick. Please."

"Will you tell us a joke? We sure could use one."

The drummer cleared his throat and nervously brushed his trousers. "Joke? I don't know any joke."

"Sure you do," Bud said. "All drummers know lots of jokes."

The drummer sighed and said, "I'd love to tell you a joke, Bud, but I couldn't risk it now. You boys come with me to Albuquerque. Have a good rest, gather up your strength, and then I'll tell you a joke. Right now you're in no condition for it. To be honest, my jokes are so good I'm afraid they might kill you."

"Ha!" said Temp.

"You think I'm kidding? I once did kill a man with a joke, Temple. I was on a train—Chicago to Kansas City—and there in the dining car I practiced my ginger talk on one of my brethren—a traveling man, like me, in the prime of his youth. Well, the ginger included one of my best jokes, which, sadly, was overheard by another, elderly gentleman, who had a weak heart and a mouthful of porterhouse steak. To put a long story short—he laughed, he cried, he choked, he died. Of laughter. He laughed himself to death. Once you've seen a man die laughing, you never forget it."

The drummer looked the boys over with a probing eye. "Why are you out here?" he asked.

"Adventure!" said Temp.

"Let me get this straight," said the drummer. "You're on your way from Oklahoma, across the godforsaken caprock, down to Roswell, up again to Santa Fe, and then back across the caprock to Oklahoma? And you've no other purpose than adventure? Boys!" he said, slapping his knee. "Get a job! Come with me to Albuquerque! I'll teach you the science of selling. Then your travels won't be for nothin'!"

He took Bud's chin in hand and examined his skull. "Hmmm, yes, by the distance between your eyes and the gentle bulge above your nose, I can see you're a good learner, and a good leader too."

He took Temple's chin. "And you. From the slope of your forehead, I can see that you are a man of great persuasive power. A bit reckless, maybe, but strong-willed. Selling's a science, and it's required me to make a careful study of the human skull and soul. Have you boys got wives?"

"I'm nine!" Bud said.

"I'm five!" Temp said.

"Yes, of course you are. I don't happen to judge a man by his size. I judge him by his character, and, of course, the shape of his pate. Have you no family at all? No mother worrying about you?"

"She's dead."

"Good!" he said. "Well, not good. But *good* because you're free. You don't have to suffer from leaving someone behind, as I do." He pulled from his vest pocket a creased and yellowed photograph of a young woman. "This is my wife, Loretta," he said. "I call her Little Lo."

"Is she very small?"

"No, quite tall, actually. But still she's my little girl. I miss her terribly."

Bud brushed his hand over one of the drummer's soft leather cases and asked, "I know what hardware is. But software?"

"Soon you'll know, my man. Soon you'll *all* know," he said, and raised his voice so that all the creatures of the desert could hear him. "It'll take the West like prairie fire."

"How?"

"Software," he said—whispering now—"is slippers. Slippers for the man and lady of the ranch, in a variety of western styles. Why should town people be the only ones with comfortable feet? It's the name, though, that's got the magic. If ranch slippers don't sell, then I'll sell petticoats or pillows and call *them* software. Eventually something will take off. Hardware's my regular line. But software's my passion. Every man needs a passion. What's yours, Temple?"

"Bugs," said Temp.

"Bud?" asked the drummer.

"Why, I . . . "

"Answer quickly! Don't think! Passion is feeling, not thought."

"Well, I . . . "

"Sorry, Bud," the drummer said, "I've got three towns to make by tomorrow and must be going. I'll give you to the count of five to come with me. Onetwothreefour. . . . No? Four and a half? Four and three quarters . . . "

Bud and Temp exchanged sad looks. "Five," the drummer said, whereupon his whole body drooped. A bead of sweat popped out above his lip as a dust particle blew in his eye. He removed his hat and fanned himself. "I'm a lone wolf," he said. He seemed to wilt before their very eyes. "I'll tell you honestly. I think I might die of loneliness. Brotherhood. That's the important thing. You two have it all in having each other. But now that I look at you, I see you're just two small boys. Have you a gun?"

Bud showed him his shotgun. "Hmmmm," said the drummer, as he peered into its rusty barrel. "I suppose you could hurt a prairie dog with this, but you'll hardly bruise a grown man if you shoot him right in the heart. Survival out here, Bud, like selling, is no joke. There's meanness in men and animals that must not be underestimated.

"Here," he said. He removed the pin from his lapel and stuck it to Bud's vest. Then he climbed back into his buggy and, as he nudged his horse away from them and headed back into the desert, he called to the boys, "Now you're honorary members of the brotherhood of United Commercial Travelers! Wherever you may be lost or in need or in danger of any kind, find one of *my* brothers, a traveling man, and he will risk life and limb to help you."

The boys followed him with their eyes as he vanished into a cloud of blustery dust. Then they patted their horses, hopped onto their saddles, and rode onward, in the direction—they hoped—of the train tracks, with yet much more desert to cross before they neared Roswell.

★ TWENTY-SEVEN ★
Who's Doin' the Catchin'?

When the sun went down, the desert grew cool and the boys began to shiver. Still in the middle of nowhere, with no trail or train track to guide them, they had no choice but to camp in the wide open. They hobbled the horses, spread out their suggans, and dug a pit for a fire. As Temp kindled some wood, Bud circled the camp—horses and all—with the horsehair rope as a kind of shield against creatures that might want to harm them.

Having taken his supper under the blankets with him, Temp fell asleep as a spoonful of beans was midair on its way to his mouth. The spoon and the bowl tumbled from his hands, spilling onto the ground, as he began softly to snore.

As Bud watched Temp sleep, it occurred to him for the very first time to wonder, *Why? Why'd Temp want to come on a trip*

to the caprock? Wouldn't he rather be home, safe in his bed, with
Catch on the rug and the girls tucking him in?

They'd been away for two weeks, and Bud had been too
busy to miss anybody, but suddenly the memory of home
throbbed in his heart. The girls would be sleeping now. In the
morning they'd gather around the table and laugh over breakfast. Johnny and little Pearlie were probably used to living
without the boys underfoot. They might even have come to
prefer it that way.

No one knew where they were. No one could protect them.
Catch 'em Alive Jack Abernathy couldn't protect them. Not
even the entire order of the United Commercial Travelers
could find them tonight.

He picked up his shotgun and looked at it. "It's a useless
toy," he said with disgust, and tossed it well beyond the circle
of the rope. "Why didn't Daddy give me a proper gun?"

The fire died down, and Bud's eyes began to droop. Just as
he was on the verge of deep sleep, he felt a faint vibration in
the earth. It was a soothing feeling, like being bounced on
your mother's knee. And it was growing stronger. He heard
something too—a distant *chug chug chug*, getting louder and
louder. His eyes popped open. He sat up and looked toward
the sound, but he saw nothing.

Then a whistle, loud and unmistakable, pierced the air. He
knew it had to be the train traveling southward toward
Roswell. He held his eye on the far horizon, and he waited.

Then another whistle, louder than before, preceded a rumbling *chug chug chug* that rattled his heart. Bright red stars—sparks from the coal box—filled the air above the horizon like fireworks. The tracks must have been only a few hundred yards away, just beyond a rise. They'd found it.

After the train passed, the earth continued to vibrate for several minutes, giving Bud the comforting feeling that they weren't alone—that they were again part of the world of men, and not the world of the desert. He lay down, and soon he was sound asleep.

They weren't at all alone. There were creatures in the night who'd felt the fall of the horses' hooves upon the earth, felt them long ago. Animals who'd known for hours that the boys would be coming to this very spot sooner or later. Creatures who'd smelled their sweat from miles away. From their burrows and holes and dens they'd tasted Temp's uneaten dinner on the breeze.

As long as the fire was burning strong, they kept away. But as it faded to embers, they ventured closer. And the first ones to get there were the wolves, who were the hungriest of all.

It was deep in the middle of the night when Sam and Geronimo grew restless. They pulled at their hobbles and snorted. Then Sam let out a bloodcurdling whinny, and finally Bud was awake. "What? What?" he said. "What, Sam? What's out there?"

He poked at the dying embers with a stick. There wasn't

enough life left in them to make a fire, but a few sparks floated up and drifted down, and in that faint trail of light, Bud saw a pair of blinking yellow eyes.

He froze. He'd seen enough wolves with his father to know exactly what kind of eyes those were. "One wolf," Bud thought, swallowing hard. "What could one wolf do against the four of us?"

He groped for the shotgun, but it was too far away. Out of the darkness there came a growl, low and steady, like a rattle in the animal's chest.

Eventually Bud found his weapon and gripped it tight. He crept back inside the rope circle. He raised the gun and popped it open to make sure the barrel was loaded. Then, in one swift fluid movement, he snapped it shut, tugged on the hammer, pulled the trigger, and discharged the bullet into the air overhead. It boomed like a cannon over the desert.

"I'm up! I'm up!" Temp said, lurching to his feet. He reeled and rubbed his eyes. "Who you shootin', Bud? Desperadoes?"

"No, Temp. I'm scaring off a wolf."

Both boys stared out into the darkness, as the boom of the shotgun faded to quiet. "I don't see 'im. You scared him away!" Temp said.

"He'll be back," Bud said, fumbling through his pack for the extra bullet. "Collect some wood and make a fresh fire," Bud ordered. "Do it fast."

"What good will that do?" Temp asked.

"I dunno," Bud said, snapping the bullet into the barrel of

his gun. "Go on, I've got you covered. Everything will be just fine."

Temp scratched his head, and then he obeyed. He grabbed his knife and scampered out of the rope circle, disappearing momentarily into the inky black night. When he reentered the circle, his arms were heaped up with wood.

In five minutes he had a blazing fire going, and the boys sat gazing through the flickering, lapping flames into the near distance. And then they saw not two yellow eyes, but more than a dozen of them, fanning out and surrounding the camp.

"Now go to sleep," Bud said, swallowing hard.

"Sleep?!"

"Go on," Bud said. "In the morning this will just seem like a dream. Don't worry. I ain't going to die with my boots off. And neither are you."

Temp scratched his head. Then he wrapped himself up in his suggans. He closed his eyes and squeezed them tight.

One pair of yellow eyes were bigger, brighter, and more intent than the others. Bud knew that they belonged to the leader of the pack—the alpha wolf. That was the one he had to worry about. When the fire died down, the alpha blinked to the others and the circle of eyes closed in. When Bud stoked the fire, the circle broadened.

"What do you want with us?" Bud asked. The alpha blinked his eyes again and pushed in closer. "Oh no you don't," said Bud, stoking the fire to a roaring blaze. He had only one bullet and couldn't afford to use it till he was sure he needed it. He'd have to keep them at bay with the fire.

Sam and Geronimo were hobbled and defenseless. Bud was the one who had to protect them all. Bud was their alpha boy now.

When his eyes adjusted to the darkness he could see the pack more clearly. The leader was big and strong, with a thick healthy coat. "Reckon I could get fifty dollars for you," Bud said to him. "But I don't know about your family here." The others had scraggly coats, and their ribs were showing. Most of them were mere youngsters. All of them, except for the alpha, looked as though they were starving.

"Do you really think I'll let you eat us?" Bud said to the alpha, glancing over at Temp, who was still pretending to sleep. "Don't you know that our father is Catch 'Em Alive Jack Abernathy?"

★ TWENTY-EIGHT ★

A Few Beans

The first time Bud went on a hunt with his father he was younger than Temp. For most of the day he and his daddy just rode Sam over the lush green prairie, while Catch and two wolf-chasing greyhounds ran well ahead, playing and prancing as dogs will do when they're free in open spaces.

It took a few hours to find a wolf to chase. Suddenly, everything changed. Bud shut tight his eyes as Jack spurred Sam to a thundering gallop, and the dogs' barking grew louder and fiercer. Soon there were terrible noises—a growing clamor of snarling, gnawing, gashing, tumbling, and scuffling. Bud braced himself for the worst. He knew there would be blood. But whose?

When they'd caught up with the dogs, his daddy stopped Sam in his tracks, tossed the reins to Bud, and hopped out of the saddle. Bud had no choice then but to open his eyes, which he did with trepidation.

There in the brush he saw Catch, the sweet family dog—"part collie, part pussycat"—snout to snout with a gray wolf that was twice his size. Catch was almost unrecognizable. There was nothing tame or meek about him then. He was as wild as any beast in nature.

Both animals' faces were twisted with savage rage, foam oozing from their mouths, their lips pulled tight across their gums, their gruesome teeth bared, their fur matted with saliva and blood. The greyhounds stood a few feet behind, their legs locked for battle, their dripping fangs gleaming in the day's quickly fading light.

And then, directly in between Catch and the wolf, stepped Bud's father. He was calmly wiggling the fingers of his right hand into a thin white glove, like a man dressing for a formal affair. The dogs instantly backed off, which was a turn of events that seemed to catch the wolf completely by surprise.

The wolf's eyes darted frantically from Catch, to the hounds, to Jack . . . and then to Jack's neck. Without the least show of preparation, the wolf leaped at Bud's daddy's throat.

Anticipating this, Jack raised his gloved hand just in time to land it in the wolf's gaping mouth. Before the animal knew what he'd swallowed, Jack had shoved his hand past the loafer's razorlike fangs and all the way to the soft, empty space behind his teeth. In a heartbeat they were both in the dust, and Bud's daddy was on top. From inside the mouth he had a secure grip on the wolf's jaw, which was now forced open and gave the animal a look of extreme shock, as if he'd just seen a ghost.

Once he'd stripped the wolf of its deadliest weapon, Jack pressed upon its chest with his knee until the animal was stunned senseless and gentled into complete submission. Then he lifted it up off the ground by the inside joint of its jaw and let the wolf dangle from his hand like a caught fish.

Sensing that the fight was over, Catch and the hounds had trotted away and were lapping water out of a nearby stream. "He's a good ninety-pounder," Jack said, "but he sure was an easy catch."

With his free hand he wired the wolf's jaw shut and slipped his catching hand out sideways. He flung the gentled creature across the front of the saddle, lifted Bud up to the rear, and climbed on between them.

That night at the campsite, the wolf slept, tied up to a tree. Catch and the greyhounds snoozed peacefully nearby. Everyone was exhausted, and the battle was long over.

Out of the silence, Bud heard a wolf pack singing in the night. Only his father slept through it. As the free, stirring chorus filled the air, the captive wolf and Catch and the hounds and Bud all awoke and, blinking into the firelight, longed for something. Their eyes were yellow, and Bud's were brown, but they all were longing for the same thing: Freedom.

Nothing in all his life had ever excited him more than the song of that wild wolf pack, until now, with the alpha out on the wide expanse of the caprock. Bud's father's passion might have been wolf-catching. It was hard for Bud to know for sure. But Bud's own passion was for the freedom of open spaces. Sitting there, guarding Temp from wolves, it seemed to Bud that he and the alpha were more alike than different.

The night passed, the fire stayed burning, the wolves pushed in, the wolves pushed out, again and again. The alpha's will never softened. But Bud's vigilance never wavered, not even for a second.

Just before dawn, Bud finally noticed the beans and bacon that Temp had spilled on the ground. "Beans and bacon," he said. He caught the alpha's eyes darting toward them too. "All this for a few beans." He shook his head, and the alpha wolf lowered his eyes in what to Bud seemed like shame, though he knew animals couldn't feel such things. By then the sun was rising.

Bud could see that there was going to be a prairie aurora, like they'd seen at the beginning of their trip. The first points of light began to pierce the horizon. Then, in a flash, the wheel spokes spread across the sky.

Bud was thrilled by the sight. He took his eyes off the alpha wolf long enough to follow one of the spokes as far as he could. When he looked back down to earth, the wolves were gone. Vanished. All that remained were their pawprints. Thousands of them dimpling the ground, stretching out in all directions. Only the camp inside the rope circle was untouched. No footprints there but Temp's. And Temp was sound asleep, and safe, and snoring softly.

★ TWENTY-NINE ★
Quenched

"Wake up, Bud."

When Bud opened his eyes a couple of hours later, Temp was kneeling beside him with a mess of pancakes. "I made you breakfast," he said, biting his lip to keep from breaking into a ridiculous smile.

The pancakes were lumpy in some places and undercooked in others. "Why, this is almost as good as the Harvey House," Bud said, which made Temp blush from head to toe.

"Ohmygosh," said Temp, as something important dawned on him. "I forgot all about my little 'roon. He'll be hungry too!" He rifled through his pack, pulled out the tin can, and peeled back the burlap. When he peered inside, his face fell flat.

He looked Bud in the eye with a stone-cold gaze and said with a voice that came from deep in his chest, "My 'roon is dead. He's just a little thing. And he's *nocturnal*. I should've left him in his own home. It was dark and lonely there, but he was safe." He solemnly plucked the poor little creature out of the tin can and buried him in the ground. It was a simple, but dignified ceremony.

"Let's go, Bud," he said when the job was done. "I want to get away from this place. Don't you?"

"I wouldn't mind."

"Is it Wednesday?" Temp asked. "The right Wednesday? Will Daddy make us go home?"

"Do you want him to?" Bud asked. "Answer honestly. It's safe at home. No wolves. No gyp."

"Home? *Heck* no, Bud! Why, we ain't hardly seen *nothin'* yet. I know you're crazy, but you ain't no fool!"

As they rode away from camp, a roadrunner zipped by and a horned lizard lumbered along and the air was filled with the trills of cactus wrens. In no time at all they met the train tracks, and as they followed them down toward Roswell, Bud fell asleep in his saddle. When at last he opened his eyes, they were making an easy crossing of the Pecos River. Bud found himself in a world that was green and fresh.

Something caught the attention of Temp's nose. He sniffed the air and puckered his face. "What's that smell, Bud?"

Bud sampled the odor and said, "Sheep." Soon they were on an emerald green pasture, and a sea of sheep was parting to let them through. A farmer spotted them as they passed by, and he shouted to a boy working in his barn—"It's them

Abernathy kids!"—whereupon the boy flew onto the back of a horse and thundered away toward Roswell.

"It's easy to find," said the farmer when Bud asked for directions. "Just stick to the train tracks. When you come to the peach orchards, you'll be less than ten miles away."

Bud and Temp turned to each other and grinned. "Excuse me, sir," said Bud, "but just what do these peach orchards look like? We don't want to miss them by accident."

"Well, Louis, there's lots of trees all lined up in rows as far as you can see, and each of the trees is pretty well drippin' with juicy peaches."

"Thank you, mister," said Temp, as he spurred Geronimo. "That's just what we thought peach orchards looked like!"

Over lush green grass they galloped, between tall bending trees, amid the crisscrossings of swallows. All the good grass made the horses feel fresh and full of pep. But when from a distance the boys saw the peach orchards, they slowed them down and forced them to walk the rest of the way in reverence.

It was picking time, and there were dozens of people out harvesting fruit. In the rows between the trees, there were bushels upon bushels toppling over with fuzzy pink fruit. "Some of them peaches are near as big as your head, Temp."

"Give 'em to me! I'll eat 'em all, Bud!"

"Excuse me, sir," Bud said to one of the men working in the orchard. "What are you going to do with all those peaches?"

"Hello, little boys," the man said. "Put them in cans, I reckon."

"No!" gasped Temp.

"That seems a shame," Bud said. "Can we buy some from you?"

"Where are you little fellas from?" the man asked. He spoke to them as if they were babies, not hardened travelers.

"Oklahoma."

"Hmmm," he said, doubtfully, as if he didn't believe them but had decided to humor them. "What brings you to Roswell, then?"

"Well," said Bud. "A few things. Adventure, I suppose."

"We come for the peaches," Temp interjected.

"You came all this way for peaches? By yourselves? No one to take care of you?"

"Bud took care of us," Temple said.

"Well, if you little boys have come all that way for a peach, I reckon you should just help yourselves." He plucked two big peaches from a tree and handed one to each of them.

They held them in their fists for a long time before they dared to take a bite. They didn't want to seem greedy, but there were two weeks of desert thirst built up in them, and they couldn't wait for long.

They punctured the flesh with their front teeth, releasing a torrent of juice that gushed down their chins. The fuzz, which at first almost put them off, mattered not at all in the eating. The meat was firm. The nectar was sweet, but not too sweet.

"Is it a miracle, Bud?"

"Reckon so, Temp. Who'd dream up such a thing, except God?"

The man gave them dozens of peaches, and as they jiggled down to Roswell they ate them all, one by one or two by two. As they munched, they sang, *"Coma ti yi youpy, youpy ya, youpy ya, coma ti youpy, youpy ya."* They were stuffed and happy beyond their wildest dreams, when suddenly they realized they'd entered the city limits.

They trotted down the center of a shady boulevard lined with cottonwood trees. They rode past houses with rose gardens in front and irrigation canals in the back. Roswell was shiny and clean and lush. The boys, unbathed since they left Oklahoma, with the dust of three states on them, felt out of place. They were desert animals now, and they didn't belong in a fine city like this.

As they neared the city center, however, Roswellians by the dozens emerged from the stores and houses. They lined the streets to welcome and cheer for them. It seemed that everyone in town was out shouting, "Abernathy kids! Hooray!"

Soon they were in front of the Grand Central Hotel, and the mayor himself was reaching up to shake their gummy hands. "Louis and Temple Abernathy," he said, "it's my honor to welcome you two great adventurers to Roswell, which is known as the 'pearl of the Pecos,' and to lay at your feet all the hospitality we have to offer. What's your first request?" he asked.

Bud said, "If it's Wednesday, please say so. If it's later, please shoot us."

The mayor seemed puzzled. "Why, yes, it's Wednesday," he said. "Been Wednesday all morning."

"Then please wire our daddy right away. Please. And tell him we made it. We're alive and well, and we're ready to keep going."

★ THIRTY ★

Roswell

The horses were swept away to be brushed and washed and properly fed, and the boys were in for a bit of pampering too. Bud and Temp were taken to their hotel room, which had indoor plumbing and a porcelain bathtub. They each had a long soak. Afterward, they were shining like new pennies. They put on clean white shirts and snapped on their celluloid collars and went to supper with some important people from town.

The mayor was there, with his wife and their nephew, a boy Bud's age named Peter Mallorie. He was dressed in a uniform, as he was a student at the military academy in town. He was only nine, but he acted like a grown-up. He didn't tuck his napkin into his collar but spread it upon his knees, and his conversation was full of words like "quite" and "somewhat."

His uncle the mayor boasted that Peter was the brightest student in his class. "It's the most famous military school in the West," said the mayor. Bud said he'd never heard of it, and immediately he wished he'd kept his mouth shut, because from that moment on it seemed that Peter disliked him.

Over supper Bud and Temple told everyone about their journey—about crossing the Red River, and gyp water, and the windmiller who flung snakes, and nearly dying in the desert, and the vinegarroon, and, of course, the wolves. Everyone gasped and laughed and shook their heads with disbelief, except for Peter. He mostly just looked mad, except for when he looked bored. He made Bud feel uncomfortable, like his sleeves were too short, or his ears were too big, or something.

Just when dessert was about to arrive, the editor of the newspaper came running in, waving a telegram, which he handed to Bud, saying, "Urgent missive!"

"What's it say, Bud?" Temp asked.

Bud swallowed hard and then read as all ears listened: "If you insist on going to Santa Fe, I will meet you there. Abernathy."

The trip was still on! Everyone at the table squealed in delight! Temp tossed his napkin into the air. The mayor pumped Bud's hand. Only Peter seemed unimpressed. He just said, "*I've* been to Santa Fe. What's so great about Santa Fe? It's *old*, you know. It's really *quite* old."

Later, as he lay in his feather bed on the verge of blissful sleep, Bud wasn't so sure what their father's telegram had meant. What would happen after he met them in Santa Fe?

Would he just spend a few days there and then leave them to make the journey home on their own, as planned? Bud hoped so. Or would he decide to ride the rest of the way back with them? Or, even worse, would his daddy say that Bud hadn't taken good enough care of Temp and insist on taking them and the horses back to Guthrie with him on the train?

Bud wanted more than anything to see the Goodnight Ranch—to talk to Charles Goodnight himself. If he couldn't get to Goodnight, why, the whole trip would be pointless. And if he couldn't get him and Temp there on his own, without his father's help, what would be the good of that?

It was the first message they'd had from their father in two weeks, though, and it made a lump rise to Bud's throat. He read it again and again. "If you insist . . . Abernathy." As he lay in the delicious comfort of his bed, he felt warm and safe in a way he did when as a boy he rode Sam with his father's arms around him. The green prairie like a cushion for Sam's hooves. The blue sky above a safeguard. And everything right in the world.

For the next two days the mayor and the newspaper editor showed the boys around town. They were extremely proud of Roswell, its nine thousand citizens and its dozens of doctors and its elaborate sewers and its sixty miles of sidewalk and its telephone system with long-distance connections reaching all the way to Amarillo. But it was the water they were proudest of—the canals and artesian wells that had turned the desert into a rose garden.

Peter tagged along, making sassy commentary. He seemed to expect Bud to join in, but Bud, to his own dismay, didn't have a sassy bone in his body. He felt quite tongue-tied around Peter, in fact, and everything he said seemed to come out flat and dull as dust.

On their last afternoon in Roswell, Peter came to the hotel and said, "You look like you could use a drink."

"We do?" Bud said.

"Come with me," said Peter, as he led them outside. He was dressed up like a mail-order cowboy. He wore brand-new fringed suede chaps, high-heeled boots without a scuff, and a big stiff Stetson hat. And he'd ridden over on a beautiful pinto pony who looked as if he got a bath every day and twice on Sundays.

Bud asked, "Where to?"

"A saloon," said Peter.

Bud snorted and said, "Aw, come on."

"Whatcha scared of? You ain't wearing knee pants. They'll give a boy a whiskey so long as his pants come down to his ankles."

"Sorry. We can't," Bud said.

"You double-distilled son of a gun," said Peter, sniffing around Bud as if he had a foul odor. "You're buggy, ain't you? You got a gun?"

"A shotgun," Bud said, instantly wishing he'd kept his mouth shut. He worried that this phony cowboy wanted to have some kind of phony cowboy showdown.

"I don't go anywhere without my pistol," Peter said. "Want to see it?" Before Bud could answer, Peter reached into his vest pocket and pulled out a little pearl-handled revolver. "Ordered it from the Sears, Roebuck catalog. Cost me two dollars fifty."

He twirled it on his finger. Round and round it went. It spun around so many times that even Peter seemed surprised. He quite lost control of it and fumbled to make it stop. When finally he caught hold of the handle he accidentally squeezed down on the trigger. And then he shot himself right in the foot—the right one—and cried like a two-year-old, the sight of which was far too embarrassing for Bud and Temp to watch.

They were not at all surprised or hurt when Peter was not among the Roswellians gathered in the streets to send the boys off on the morning of their departure. But everyone else was there, it seemed. Sam and Geronimo were looking as fit as ever when the liveryman brought them over to the hotel. Their saddles and bridles gleamed. Their stirrups were glistening.

After giving Temp a leg up, the newspaper editor shook his head and said, "Little fellow, you look about like a wide turtle out on a log in a large stream."

High above the crowd on their spiffed-up horses, the boys waved to all the assembled citizens of Roswell as if each and every one was their very best friend. They were rested and fat and happy to be trail-bound again. Their saddlebags were lumpy with peaches and a pound bag of candy, which Temp had bought for fifteen cents.

With the knowledge that they were smarter at least than the brightest boy in the best military school, and with a refreshing odor of soap about them, they headed out into a brand-new landscape of foothills and arroyos, and they wondered what the mountains would look like when at last they loomed on the horizon. And just how old *was* Santa Fe? More than a hundred years?

★ **THIRTY-ONE** ★

The Jackass

Before leaving Roswell, they sent a telegram to their father. Bud had never written a telegram before, so he copied the one they got from Jack: "If you insist on going to Santa Fe, we will meet you there in three days. Abernathys."

"Will we tell Daddy about the vinegaroon when we see him?" Temp asked, as they began the journey to Santa Fe.

"It's an awful sad story, Temp."

"Do you think maybe Daddy will ride with us awhile, Bud?"

Bud hesitated before saying, "You want him to, Temp?" He wasn't sure he wanted to know the answer.

"Sure I do, Bud. That'd be bully!"

"Well," said Bud, weakly, "I don't think Daddy could ever say no to you, if you asked him to come along."

"Hmmm," said Temp, thinking it over. "I suppose he could

look after us. Right, Bud? In case we got caught by some more wolves or somethin'."

"Yep," said Bud, though it hurt him to hear that Temp wanted someone else to look after him. "But, Temp," he said, "I reckon that from now on things will be easy. A regular picnic. I reckon the hard times are behind us and we don't really need to take Daddy away from the girls and his job as U.S. Marshal."

"Hmmm," said Temp. "Somethin' to think about, huh, Bud?"

Unfortunately, their thinking was cut short by some nasty business brewing with the weather. In the brief time since they'd left Roswell, the sky had turned from blue to gray and now to black. The horizons tightened around them like a fist. When a lightning bolt split the sky in two, the crack of thunder sent the horses shrieking and rocking back on their heels.

The lightning was so powerful that somehow it caused sparks to fly right out of the horses' ears. Bud and Temp didn't mind a little rain, but neither boy had ever seen *that* before, and it gave them both a start. When hailstones started falling out of the sky by the barrelful, they jumped down and crawled underneath the horses' bellies for a powwow.

"I think I saw a cave up ahead," said Bud. "Or at least I hope I did. I say we fly like the wind. I don't like the way these horses are electrifyin'."

The boys got back in their seats and made haste to the cave. It was just a small hole in a big rock, with barely enough room for all four of them, but it would have to do.

With each lightning strike the cave filled with an eerie glow, then went black as ink. Every time a thunderbolt cracked like fireworks overhead, they felt the explosion in their chests. The horses were unsettled and scratched nervously at the ground. It was a long, wet day and a hard, cold night that followed. Their feather beds in Roswell were faint but aching memories.

As they waited out the storm, they had themselves a lunch of peaches and candy. "This what you meant by a 'regular picnic,' Bud?" asked Temp. For dinner they had some more peaches and candy. For breakfast the next morning, by which time the sky at last had cleared, they ate only candy, having run out of peaches.

By then Temp was drunk on sugar and babbling away a mile a minute. "Will Daddy be happy to see us, Bud? You think he'll hug us? Or just shake our hands? Do you suppose I've grown? Do you think Daddy will think I'm bigger, Bud? When will I be as big as you, Bud? This cave sure is smelly, ain't it?"

Bud was delighted to leave the confines of their cave and to get back in the saddle. As they hit the trail, the air was soft and sweet, alive with the songs of spadefoot toads and the smell of wet greasewood. Soon the sun dried up the mud, and Sam kicked up an enormous plume of dust that all but obliterated Temp from Bud's view.

At noon they arrived at a farm owned by a family called

Hurlburt, all of whom were lined up and waiting for them beside a great big table laid out with white linen cloth and real china dishes. "You're right on time," Mrs. Hurlburt said.

"Excuse me?" Bud said. "Are you expectin' someone?"

"Why, we're expecting *you*," said Mrs. Hurlburt. "When I see dust rising on the horizon in the morning, it's a fair bet we'll have visitors at noon. From the size of the dust cloud I figured you to be small. But not *this* small. You're just a couple of whistles!"

They sat down to a delicious meal with delightful company. Every story told at the table was an occasion for an uproarious laughter that in itself was very amusing. The Hurlburts all laughed in a way that sounded like *hee-haw hee-haw hee-haw.*

When it was time to leave, the boys were sad to go. "This is a nice farm," Temple said. "What do you grow here, anyway?"

"A bit of sorghum," said Mr. Hurlburt. "But mostly mules."

Without stopping to think before he spoke, Temp said, "Ain't mules stupid, though?" Bud gave him a kick, and the Hurlburts all blinked at him dumbly, as if they hadn't understood a word he said.

"Which reminds me," said Mr. Hurlburt. "If you see any horses in the next several miles, stay clear and give them lots of room. We've got ten herds of breeding mares, and each herd has its own jackass with 'em. In case you don't know, breeding a jackass and a horse makes a mule. And jackasses don't like strangers, especially ones who think their babies are stupid."

"Um," said Temp. "I was just *kiddin*! I love jacks. I oughta. My daddy's a Jack! I ain't afraid of *him*."

The whole family broke out into a chorus of hee-haws. "Honest, boys," said Mr. Hurlburt. "You've had enough trouble, ain't ya? Those beasts ain't as nice as your daddy. They'd just as soon eat you as look at you. And your hat and your spurs and your boots and your brother."

It was a beautiful day, though, and such a nice farm to ride across that the boys forgot to worry. "I reckon the rest of the ride will be a breeze, Temp," said Bud, as they loped away laughing like Hurlburts—"hee-haw hee-haw."

"Wait for us, Bud!" he heard Temp call.

But Sam was feeling fit and fast and wouldn't hear the word "whoa." Bud got well ahead. He and Sam flew over the pasture and charged up a steep rise, and when they got to the top they stumbled directly upon a herd of horses.

"Uh-oh," said Bud.

Twenty doe-eyed mares—all chomping on grass and blinking kindly at him—spread apart to reveal, in the very middle of the herd, a stocky jackass who was none too happy to have his grass munching interrupted. Without even batting an eye, the jack tore at Bud. But Sam was far too fast for him. The jack soon gave up and was heading back to his girlfriends when Temp and Geronimo came lumbering up the rise.

"Buuuuuuuuuud! Look at me! No hands!" called Temp. "I'm flyin'! Hee-haw hee-haw hee-haw." The jack's eyes widened with evil pleasure at the sight of Temple standing in his stirrups, flapping his arms and pointing his chin to the sky. The jack snorted, brayed, and scratched at the dirt.

"Look out!" cried Bud.

When at last Temp looked, the jack was already barreling toward him in a cloud of dust and fury, and it appeared to be too late to get out of his way. "Wha? Who? How?" stuttered Temp. "Glang! Giddap!" He kicked at Geronimo frantically, but the horse was oblivious to the danger and in no mood to be hurried. It wasn't till the jack was so close that they could almost feel his hot breath that Geronimo got the picture and jumped straight up into the air. His feet scampered beneath him before he got to galloping.

Geronimo's legs pumped and pumped, but the jack was gaining fast. "Bud!" cried Temp. "Help!"

When Temp glanced behind him and saw the jack's big teeth clacking wildly just a few yards from his rear end, he freed his feet from the stirrups, shimmied out of his saddle, and scrambled forward onto Geronimo's neck. Then he started hysterically screaming, "Daddy! Daddy!"

It broke Bud's heart to hear it. He'd never seen Temp so scared before. He couldn't just sit there watching Temp's bottom get chewed off, so he galloped Sam over to him and quirted Geronimo's hind legs. "C'mon, boy, you can do it," he hollered.

"I'm a goner," shouted Temp over the thundering of hooves. "This time, for keeps!" The dust they were kicking up was blinding. It wasn't till the very last moment that Bud was able to see that they were fast approaching a fence. By then it was too late to change their course. They'd have to jump. Or crash.

As a gust of wind cleared away the dust, Bud spotted a gate. The jack was getting ready to lunge for Temp's flesh. This was it. Do or die.

Bud spurred Sam ahead toward the fence and, at the last possible moment, he leaped out of his saddle. With his feet barely touching the ground, he was heaved into the gate, which he managed to unlatch and open in time to let Sam through. "Come on, Temp!" he yelled.

He couldn't bear to watch. The jack's eyes were brimming with wicked satisfaction as he stretched wide his jaw and readied himself for the taste of human meat.

Temp had a survivor's instinct, though, and some kind of crazy nerve. With the gate in sight, he spurred Geronimo and willed him to gallop faster.

Temp and Geronimo flew through the gate. Just as Bud shut it behind them the jack came crashing into it with the full force of his furious body, causing it to shudder and nearly to topple.

The fence stretched all the way back to the ranch house, where Mr. Hurlburt, seeing its reverberations, shook his head and said to his wife, "Jack got them boys, I reckon. Whenever will their troubles end?"

★ THIRTY-TWO ★
A Brite Hors

In the course of their adventures, Sam had taken to Bud as he'd taken to only one other man in his life—Jack. Bud could make Sam spin on a dime just by wishing it. Sitting in his saddle felt perfect. If Bud fell asleep on the trail, Sam saw to it he wasn't jostled or jolted. If Bud slept too late in the morning, Sam woke him by gently nickering and nibbling at his ear with his velvety lips. It was a fine way to wake up. Sam was a fine horse. He might have been the very finest.

Bud often thought that if anything ever happened to Sam—if he got hurt or lost or stolen or killed—he wouldn't be able to go on. He'd probably have to quit school and go work for Charles Goodnight. He'd bury his sorrows in the emptiness of the caprock.

Temp and Geronimo had made their bonds too. Geronimo

was no Sam. He couldn't outrun a steam engine or outwit a wolf, as Sam could do, with his eyes closed, but he'd proven himself to be a sensitive creature and a good friend. When Temp's ankles got swollen, Geronimo took to limping, too, out of sympathy. When Temp was happy, Geronimo's step was brisk and buoyant. When Temp was tired, Geronimo dragged.

The horses took good care of the boys, as they did of each other, and all they required in return was some fresh water and a handful of oats now and again. If there was some good grass to munch on, all the better. Bud often thought how horses were among the most powerful animals on earth, and yet their needs were so few. They took little from the land and gave so much to mankind.

On the trail, Bud had a lot of time to work out his philosophies of life. The grandeur of the land, the nobility of the native animals, and the companionship of horses tended to make him even more philosophical than usual.

When the purple Rockies began to loom beyond the plains, Sam and Geronimo sensed the boys' gasping, and they stopped to allow them to contemplate the view. Having lived always in Oklahoma, a state not made famous by its few modest mountain ranges, Bud and Temp were flatlanders. They'd had no way of imagining just how majestic mountains could be.

"How's Daddy gettin' up there, Bud?"

"Train."

"How's a train gettin' up there, Bud?"

"Don't rightly know, Temp. Seems impossible. But I reckon he might be speeding across the caprock right about now, heading to Santa Fe."

Another day's riding and they were enveloped in mountains with no time to wonder or marvel at them. Up the steep trail the horses labored, uncomplaining, as rocks rolled away under hoof and plummeted into nothingness. As the air got thinner, heads began to swim and stomachs to grumble.

They nooned by a stream and had some lunch. They ought to have saved some of their provisions for later, but there wasn't much, and they were voracious. They ate every last morsel of beans and bacon and polished off their one remaining can of tomatoes. The horses ate every last bit of oats. And then there was nothing left.

"But I'm still hungry, Bud," said Temp. Judging by the way he was pawing at the empty tin of oats, Geronimo was still hungry too.

"Just another day and a half and we'll be at the governor's mansion, eating roast beef and pie. Hard times are over, Temp."

"I can't wait a day and a half! I'm starving, Bud."

"Don't worry. We'll come to a town soon. I tell you what: Next general store we find, I'll get you some strawberry pop."

The horses drudged on, though their stomachs were empty and their spirits were drooping. Much to Bud's dismay, no town appeared, and before they knew it, night was falling fast.

When they came to a place where the land seemed to flatten out, near a stream not much wider than a scratch, Bud decided they had no choice but to stop and camp.

"I'm sorry, Temp," he said, but "sorry" wasn't a tenth of what he was. "I suggest we go straight to sleep. Otherwise we'll just think about food. Tomorrow when we're feasting at the governor's mansion, this will all seem like a dream."

"You think if I try," Temp said, "I can make myself dream about Daddy?"

"Sure you can. Just close your eyes and try to picture him."

Bud tried to sleep, but he couldn't. He stayed awake listening for sounds of misery. The slightest rustling of hobbles made Bud worry that the horses were suffering. Seeing Temp clutching his gut made Bud think the very worst of himself. This was all his fault.

He didn't care at all about his own grumbling stomach. But the thought that Temp and Sam and Geronimo were wanting for food was more than he could bear. The night was deep, and the silence was deafening. He wanted to throw his arms around Sam's neck and beg his forgiveness.

As he lay there, tossing and turning, his fears grew larger than life. They seemed as big, as dark, and as mysterious as the mountains. "This is no good," he said. He got up and had a walk around.

He stepped over the stream and through some pinyons and soon found himself scrambling up a steep incline where, tucked between two trees, he found a wooden cross that someone had planted in a bare patch of dirt. The sun had begun to rise, and he could just make out the words that had been carved deep into the wood.

HERE LIES

FIREFLY

A BRITE HORS

WHOSE FLAME DIED RITE HERE SEPT 3, 99

"These mountains are a graveyard for horses," Bud said to himself as it dawned on him that six feet below lay the remains of a once-beloved creature named Firefly.

It was a disturbing thought, and Bud wasted no time in shaking free of it. He slid on his bottom back to the camp, where he busied himself cleaning up and readying the horses for the trail. "I'm sorry, Temp," he said. "I'm sorry you're hungry. Now, wake up, and let's find someone to feed us. Let's get you and the horses to Daddy."

THIRTY-THREE

Santy Fe

Governor Curry's brand-new brick mansion could be seen over the roofs of Santa Fe's little adobe cottages from almost a mile away. The boys didn't notice the ancient buildings or the burros clogging the roads or the Navajo Indians milling about the plaza. They had their minds set on getting fed. When they arrived at the mansion, they were delirious with hunger and sick from the heights.

A young boy appeared at the front door and began speaking to them, but Bud and Temp had a hard time understanding him. He was dark-skinned, about seven years old, and he had an unfamiliar accent. "You are the Abernathy kids, yes?" he said. "Governor Curry says please come in and rest while I see to your horses. He will be home within the hour to have supper with you. Your daddy sent a telegram saying he will come soon."

As they followed him in, Temp looked at the boy suspiciously. There was something about him he found vexing and untrustworthy.

"Oh," said the boy, "and I'm meant to say: 'Welcome to Santy Fe.'"

The house smelled of baking bread and roasting meat and some kind of pie. It didn't matter what kind of pie it was. Any pie, any pie at all, was their greatest wish, their deepest desire. They hadn't eaten for a day and a half. They could not wait an hour for supper. They could not wait another minute. "Please feed us now," said Bud.

"Please," said Temp. "Whoever you are . . . please."

The boy looked at them piercingly, then he waved at them to follow him into the kitchen, where a cook was preparing the evening meal. "Sit," the boy said. "I suppose you can have your baths later. I'm J.P., by the way."

Bud and Temp were fed fresh bread, roast beef, potatoes, and peach pie, and then they were fed all over again, though they passed on seconds of pie. They'd had quite enough peaches already. While they ate, wordlessly, J.P. kept an eye on them. There was still something about J.P. that Temp didn't trust, so he engaged him in a staring contest to see what he was made of.

"What kind of Indian are you?" Temp asked, expressionlessly, his eyes unblinking.

"No kind," said J.P., his stare unwavering. "I'm Filipino."

"Stop pulling my leg," said Temp. "That's a kind of horse, ain't it?"

"Maybe you're thinking of a palomino," said J.P. "A Filipino comes from the Philippines."

"Oh," said Temp, who had never before even heard of the Philippines. He blinked, but he didn't drop his stare. "That's what I thought."

"Governor Curry used to be the head of police in the Philippines," said J.P., "and he brought me here to educate me. Before that he was a Rough Rider. Do you know about the Rough Riders, Temple?" He had an itch on his cheek, and he scratched it. But he didn't blink.

"Of course I do."

"They were the soldiers led by Teddy Roosevelt in the Spanish-American War, before he became president."

"I know that," said Temp.

"I've met Teddy Roosevelt."

"Me too."

"When I grow up, I want to work for the United States government," said J.P.

"I want to be a traveling salesman," said Temp.

"You do?" asked Bud, his mouth full of mashed potatoes. It was the first he'd heard of it.

"Hmmmm," said J.P. "That's very interesting."

Later that night they sat in the parlor with Governor Curry, swapping stories about gyp water and wolves and the Philippines and the Rough Riders. J.P. listened, quietly, from a corner of the room, studying the boys carefully. The governor was a funny sort of man, who liked to tease and tell tales and to hear them too.

"But enough about me," he said. "I want to talk about you. You're clever boys, and we've seen that you're tough enough to lick vinegarroons and rattlesnakes and mean jackasses, and you've got nerves to match those of a hungry wolf. But what about vicious men? Would you know an outlaw if you saw one?"

"I reckon *so*," said Temp. "I ought to. I've only seen about a thousand of 'em on posters in my daddy's office."

"Is that right?" the governor said. "And what about that horse of yours? Isn't he an outlaw?"

"Sam Bass?" asked Bud, perplexed.

The governor sang:

> *"Sam Bass was born in Indiana,*
> *it was his native home,*
> *And at the age of seventeen*
> *young Sam began to roam."*

"Isn't that your Sam Bass? The one that song was written about?" the governor asked. "The same Sam Bass who robbed trains and banks and terrorized the land?"

"Sam's named after that man," Bud said. "But that man was a *good* badman. He gave the money he stole to the poor."

"A good badman? Does one exist?" asked the governor.

"And how could you tell the difference? Hmmm . . . What if I told you that here in this very house there was someone who had been in prison? Charged with sixteen crimes and misdemeanors? Which of the people in this house would you suppose that is?"

Bud thought about all the servants he'd met, who did the cleaning and cooking and office work. But Temp didn't have to think twice. "It's *J.P.*," he blurted out, pointing his finger. "For sure it's *J.P.*"

"Me!?" cried J.P.

"Now, now," said the governor. "J.P. is probably the least criminal person in this house. He's a good boy and never misses church. What if I said it was me? I'm the villain."

"You're joking," Bud said.

"Am I? The truth is that in my youth I was arrested, Bud, for deeds I did not commit. But all I'm saying is you can't be too careful. Good men can look like bad men. And vice versa. Where you're going from here there are lots of caves and other good hiding places, where the meanest kinds of men conceal themselves from the law. Bandits, bank robbers, cattle rustlers, and—the very lowest of them all—*horse thieves*. Horse thieves who'd love to get their hands on that Sam Bass of yours, I promise you. Tell me, Bud," the governor continued. "Would you use that fire stick of yours—that shotgun—on a man if you had to?"

"I reckon I would."

"I'm not so sure," said the governor.

Temp had heard enough. "Bud is the bravest boy there ever was," he said. "He's not afraid of nothin'. He took care of me, didn't he? He'd shoot a man, all right, if he had to. If he met you when you were a criminal, he would have licked you too. If I could have Buffalo Bill or Louis Abernathy, I'd take Bud. I don't suppose there's anyone braver in all the world. I can't think of nobody. No one at all. Can you think of anyone, Bud? Can you? Can you? There's no one!"

Bud's heart was just about bursting from his chest, when suddenly a familiar voice rang from the front door: "Is anybody home!?" Bold footsteps could be heard resounding through the hallways, and then Jack Abernathy appeared in the room, his eyes sparkling and his arms outspread.

"Catch 'Em Alive Jack!" said the governor. "You're early, but you're just in time to settle an argument. We were just debating who is the bravest man in this house. I say it's you. Temp here says otherwise."

"Look at 'em," exclaimed Jack. "From the looks of you two, I'd say you boys have been on a luxury cruise. Are you sure you've been banging around the caprock all these weeks? Come here and throw yourselves at your old dad."

"Oh, Daddy," exclaimed Temp, as he dove into his father's arms. "Oh, Daddy, what did we do without you?"

★ THIRTY-FOUR ★
The Road to Las Vegas

During the couple of days they stayed in Santa Fe, J.P. showed the boys the sights, and Jack often tagged along. Temp stuck to his father like an extra arm, whispering in his ear and telling him all their stories about wolves and jackasses and near-starvation and thirst and exhaustion. Seemed it was always Temp and Jack, Jack and Temp, with Bud just a little bit on the outside of things and wondering when he and Temp would be getting back on the trail toward Goodnight Ranch.

J.P. took to chatting with Bud as they toured the town. "Santa Fe is three hundred years old," said J.P.

"That right?" said Bud.

"I learned that in school. Will you be home in time for school?" J.P. asked him.

Bud hadn't thought about school since leaving Guthrie.

The very idea of it felt like an arrow piercing his heart. "I reckon so," said Bud with an eye on Jack and Temp, who were giggling together like a couple of schoolgirls. "But I'm thinkin' of cuttin' out on school anyway. Thinkin' of going to work for Charles Goodnight." He surprised J.P. by saying it, but he surprised himself more.

J.P. asked incredulously, "You mean you don't like school?"

Before Bud could answer, Jack was requiring his attention. "Look here, Bud and Temp," he said. "You should know that I came here to take you home with me on the train tomorrow." Bud's heart sank.

"But hearing all your stories," he continued, "I got to thinking it's been far too long since I've had a good old-fashioned boyish adventure of my own. What say we ride together awhile?"

This news delighted Temp. "Ain't it great, Bud?" he said, throwing his arms around his daddy's neck.

"Yep," said Bud. "Great." But he didn't exactly mean it.

It was soon decided that Jack would accompany the boys from Santa Fe, across the Glorietta Pass, to the New Mexican town of Las Vegas, a place renowned in earlier times for its lawlessness and violence, where Temp hoped to see a shootout or a barroom brawl. Jack secured for the ride the loan of a horse from Governor Curry—a puddin'-footed mare named Princess.

"Imagine me ridin' somethin' called Princess into Las Vegas," Jack whispered to Bud. "But what am I to do? It's

wrong to look a gift horse in the mouth, as everyone knows."
He glanced wistfully at Sam. "Don't suppose *you'd* like to give
young Princess a try, eh, Bud? She's a nice-looking black mare.
That blaze on her forehead looks to me like a bow and arrow."

Bud said, "Do I have to, Daddy?" The pain on his face was
glaring. Jack couldn't bear to look at him.

"Oh, all right," he said. "You and your buddy Sam stick
together. What's it matter who I ride, anyway? I'm just a U.S.
Marshal is all."

As they left Santa Fe, Jack tried to take the lead position,
but it turned out that Princess wasn't the kind of horse who
liked to be boss. As Sam wasn't the kind of horse to let another
horse be boss, it wasn't long before he was nudging past her
and taking his rightful place as leader. Geronimo wasn't going
to ride with his nose in a strange girl horse's behind, so he
passed her up, too, and took his accustomed position right
behind Sam.

That left Jack on Princess tailing the group, losing ground,
and none too happy about it. Jack wasn't exactly the kind of
man content to take up the rear. At the first town they came
to, he said to Bud, "Sorry, son, this ain't gonna work."

Bud sighed, hopped out of Sam's saddle, and handed over
the reins. "Come on, boys," Jack said, making himself comfortable on his old wolf-hunting horse and trotting on ahead.
"Let's get to Las Vegas in time to have supper at the Harvey
House."

"Yes, sir!" squealed Temp, trotting along after him.

It took Bud a while to get situated on Princess. While he fumbled with the stirrups, the others got well ahead and didn't seem to notice that Bud was missing, or to care. From where Bud sat, it looked as if Sam was plenty happy to have his old master on his back.

As Princess plodded along, the trail ahead wrapped around the mountain, and Temp and Jack disappeared from sight. Bud could hear them singing, "*Coma ti yi youpy, youpy ya, youpy ya, coma ti youpy, youpy ya.*" But their voices quickly grew faint. Soon Bud was completely on his own. Alone. A lone wolf. And he immediately got to feeling sorry for himself.

"If Temp wants to stick with Daddy, that's just fine," he said to Princess. As it turned out, Princess was a pretty good listener. Anyway, there wasn't anyone else to talk to, not for miles and miles and miles.

"I don't need him," Bud continued. "I'll go to Goodnight Ranch on my own. Might even stay," he said. "Might never leave."

Bud was so lost in his own misery that he barely noticed that the trail was getting narrower. At times it was hardly a trail at all. Sometimes it seemed as if the entire gigantic mountain was leaning against his left shoulder, while to the right there was nothing but the thinnest air.

Every now and then, a voice would be carried to him on a breeze. Temp's little laugh would bounce against the mountain and hit Bud smack in the face. He peered down into the abyss to his right in hopes of spotting him, but all that he saw was a prison chain gang building a road a few hundred feet below. He felt closer to those prisoners than he did to his own father and brother.

He nooned alone, resting with Princess on a ledge that overhung a chasm. As hawks looped overhead, he imagined himself traveling on to Goodnight Ranch without Temp. Self-pity bloomed in his chest like a thorny rose. It stung, but it was beautiful.

He and Princess carried on toward Las Vegas, and when finally the trail opened up and meandered into town, he half expected to find Temp and his father waiting for him. But there was no sign of them anywhere. "They'll be finished with their meal already, Princess," said Bud, "and there won't be nothing left for me."

When Bud found the Harvey House restaurant, Temp was sitting on Jack's lap and the two of them were as thick as thieves, laughing and whispering.

"Bud!" Jack exclaimed. "Hello, Princess! Temp here was worried about you, but I told him you'd find us. Come here and eat your supper before it gets cold." A sirloin steak with mashed potatoes and a bowl of Mexican soup were waiting for him at the table.

"I'm just telling Temp how Las Vegas used be in the old days," Jack said. "Used to be a windmill right in the middle of the town square, and they'd hang folks from it when they were bad."

"Is that right?" said Bud, dismally, as he sat down and carved into his steak. He imagined a rope around his neck and wondered if anyone would care if he was hanging from that windmill.

"Yep," said Jack. "Those were the excitin' days, I reckon, but they're long gone. Ain't no more desperadoes in these parts. Now, listen, boys," he said. "There's a train leaving tonight for home. What do you say we take it? What do you say, Bud? Temp here was just telling me how he's always wanted to see a Pullman car. Isn't that right, Temp?"

"Um," said Temp.

"C'mon, you boys. You've had enough, ain't you? How much more can two boys take?"

"Daddy," Temp said, "won't you ride with us to Goodmorning Ranch and show us around there?"

"Aw, Temp," said Jack. "My bottom's sore already. Turns out I don't have the skin for trail riding anymore. Anyway, school starts in less than a week, and you boys need to rest up and get ready for it."

Bud's heart was breaking. Did his father really think he was a quitter? And why'd he have to go mention school for? "If Temp wants to go home with you," he said, "it's all right by me. I still want to make the Goodnight Ranch, though. I don't mind going alone."

"You don't, Bud?" asked Temp, meekly. "You want to get rid of me? Why, we ain't hardly seen nothin' yet."

"No," Bud said. "I just thought you wanted to go home with Daddy."

"No, Bud, I don't. I want to finish the trip. I want to see

Goodmorning Ranch. Please don't make me go home, Bud. We ain't done everything yet."

"It's Good*night* Ranch, Temp," said Bud. He had to bite his lip to keep from smiling. Then both boys turned their most heartbreaking sad-dog expressions on their father, who promptly caved in.

"Oh, boys," said Jack, "do you have any idea what kind of grief I'm going to get if I go home without you? Do you have any idea?"

"Daddy," said Bud, "I know it seems as if we've been going a long time and that we must be tired of traveling. But there's just one more place we need to see before we go home. We're not ready to end it just yet. Not just yet."

★ **THIRTY-FIVE** ★
Trigger Happy

Soon Princess was on a train back to Santa Fe, and Jack was speeding home across the caprock. It was a new day, and the boys were on their own again. Bud was back on Sam, joyfully singing,

> *"A cowboy's life is a dreary, dreary life,*
> *some say it's free from care."*

As Temp was singing,

> *"A cowboy's mite is a deary deary mite,*
> *some say its flea is fair."*

After a steep downhill ride, during which every step was a labor for the horses, they eventually landed in the low foothills, where the riding was easier. It was a funny sort of place, though. Not the sort of place where people lived or worked or raised children. The trail itself sometimes disappeared altogether, and there was nothing to mark the land but caves and rocky outcroppings, and no fellow travelers but birds of prey gliding overhead.

And yet the boys couldn't shake the feeling that they were being watched.

"You feel that, Temp?"

"Feels like eyes, Bud."

As the sky grew dusky, the strange feeling got stronger. They heard rustlings among the trees, which sounded like the scampering of feet. They sometimes thought they smelled gunpowder. But whenever they turned to look, there was no one to be seen.

Then they heard a sound that was unmistakably a burp. Not just a little burp but a great big deep smelly belch. Bud and Temp stopped and looked around. There was no one there.

"You hear that belch, Temp?"

"It was worse than one of Daddy's. Hey, Bud," Temp said. "You don't suppose Daddy's following us, making sure we're safe, do ya?"

"No, Temp. We put him on that train ourselves."

The feeling of eyes got stronger as night fell. Chills traveled up and down their spines. When they came to the banks of the Canadian River, they followed it eastward in hopes of finding a safe, smooth place to camp out.

A little later, Bud spotted what looked like a simple frame house tucked into some rocks and trees. "Smell that?" he said. "Pinyon fire. Someone's cooking."

They pushed their way through the trees toward the house. It was a simple wooden house, so newly built that there were still shavings on the ground. Outside there was a blazing campfire, and beside it a side of beef waiting to be cooked. It was dim and quiet, with no sound or movement but the flickering of the fire, and the boys didn't notice that there were a dozen motionless fellows standing silently among the trees, watching them. Their dark clothes blended into the night air and made them resemble trees themselves. Each one had a hand on his holster. Not a muscle twitched.

Until one of them belched. "Sorry," he said, covering his mouth.

Someone else snuck up on the boys from behind. "Hello, young fellers," he said, startling the boys and the horses both. "Sorry, didn't mean to booger you."

He was a good-looking man, younger than their father, with long, shiny blond hair pulled back in a ponytail. He had a big bright smile that twinkled in the firelight. Something about his white shiny teeth mesmerized the boys. They couldn't help themselves smiling back at him in a dopey sort of way. Something about him was familiar and instantly put them at ease.

"You lost?" he asked.

"We're heading to Texas," said Bud. "To the Goodnight Ranch."

"Huh," said the fellow. His smile faded fast. "What you wanna go there for?"

"Goodnight's a friend of our daddy," said Temp.

"That right?" said the fellow, distastefully, as if he'd eaten something rotten. "And what's your daddy's name?"

"Jack Abernathy," said Temp. "U.S. Marshal for Oklahoma."

"Huh," the man said again. The taste in his mouth seemed to be making him sick now. He looked as though he might vomit. "Jack Abernathy," he snorted, the name of their father coming out of his mouth like spit.

After a moment's quiet reflection, though, his face turned bright again. As quickly as if he'd lit a match, he flashed his dazzling smile. "He let you come out here by yourselves?"

"Yes, sir," said Bud.

"Why?"

Bud had to think about it. He didn't rightly know. "I guess 'cause we wanted to."

"Well," said the man, "now, *that's* a reason. You almost have to respect a man who'd let his little boys go travelin' just 'cause they want to." He slapped Bud on the back in a brotherly way and laughed. At that, all the other fellows started laughing too. Their hands fell from their holsters and they went back to their business of cooking supper and tending a dozen or so

cattle that the boys now could see were straggling along the
river's edge. The fellow who belched before did it again.

"My name's A—" the blond shiny fellow said, stopping
midsentence. After some thought he said, "Why, it's . . .
Arizona. That's right. That's what it is. That's a good name,
ain't it? And I'll be your friend for life, if you'll be mine. These
fellers here are all my brothers. They're not real brothers, like
you two. I'm not so lucky as you. They're more like honorary
brothers. And you can be one, too, if you like. Would you?
Please?"

"Heck, yes," said Temp. His eyes were full of sodden admi-
ration for this Arizona. He was smitten.

"Good. So long as you're with us, no harm can come to
you. How 'bout you eat a bean with us, eh? And spend the
night, and joke and wrestle a bit? Hmm? We've got this big
house, and it feels kind of empty without any children in it."

"Thank you," said Bud.

Arizona's brothers were just about the friendliest folk Bud
and Temp had ever met. Some of their names were Shorty and
Slimey and Sneaky and Trigger and Slick and Smith and
Weston.

Arizona said that he and his brothers were "independent
cattlemen." They didn't much like the big outfits, like the
Goodnight Ranch. "All them big ones just get after all us little
ones," Arizona said, picking some gristle out of his teeth. "And
it ain't fair."

"That's right!" said Trigger, the fella with the belching problem.

"But if you want to be a friend to Mr. Goodnight, I won't hold it against you," Arizona said. "'Cause I like you boys."

"That's a fine hoss," Trigger said to Bud, sneaking up behind him. "Ain't nobody ever tried to steal it?"

"Heck no," said Bud.

"I'm just saying," Trigger said, "if I was a hoss thief—which I'm *not* and never would *be*—I'd steal this hoss. It's a compleement."

"Now, Trigger," said Arizona. "You know there ain't nothin' lower in this world than a horse thief. Don't go wishin' the boys meet one."

All the other fellows agreed, most vehemently. The boys could tell that they really hated horse thieves.

Trigger took hold of the horses' reins and made to take them away. When Bud moved to stop him, Trigger said, by way of explanation, "I'm the hoss wrangler. I look after the remoother." Bud reckoned he meant he looked after the remuda, which was the cowboy word for a herd of cow horses.

Trigger's face spread into a broad smile consisting of approximately seven yellow teeth and one fake one, which appeared to be made of gunmetal. He said, reassuringly, "I'll water and brush 'em and feed 'em and love 'em. Don't worry. And I'll look after your things too." He clutched their saddlebags to his chest and nabbed Bud's shotgun right out of his hands. "Don't you worry about nothin'. We're all brothers here."

After supper, the boys carried their suggans and their saddles inside the house, where all the men were bedding down for the night. It was just a one-room shack full of crates and blankets and saddles, which the men used for pillows.

"Ain't it a nice house, Bud?" said Temp. "Ain't it cozy?"

The boys found themselves a spot near Arizona on which to make themselves a bed. Then all the fellows lay on their backs, staring at the ceiling and talking things over in the dark.

"You fellers go to school?" asked Arizona.

"Yep," said Bud, "'fraid so."

The men all moaned. "Poor feller," someone said. "Aw, what a shame."

"What about the little one?" someone asked.

"I'll start on the seventh of September," Temp said.

The fellows all groaned miserably. "Can't we keep him?" someone asked. "Can't we save him from goin' to school?"

"Now, now," Arizona said. "A boy needs his dad. Feller's got to go back to his father," and the name again came out like spit, "Catch 'Em Alive Jack Abernathy."

Arizona was bothered by noises outside and seemed to be restless. He didn't stay lying down for long but soon began pacing between one wall and the door. He poked his head out into the night and looked around numerous times, nervously, but Bud couldn't imagine what he was worried about.

Certainly no bad men or horse thieves could find them out there.

As the boys fell asleep, though, Arizona grew calm. He stood over Bud and Temp, his bright smile hanging like a half-moon above their heads. And he sang them a soft lullabye:

> *"Sam Bass was born in Indiana,*
>> *it was his native home,*
> *And at the age of seventeen*
>> *young Sam began to roam.*
> *Sam first came out to Texas*
>> *a cowboy for to be*
> *A kinder-hearted fellow*
>> *you seldom ever see."*

★ **THIRTY-SIX** ★
Watched

It wasn't easy saying good-bye to such a friendly bunch of men. But the boys had to be off, and so they hit the trail at dawn. As they followed the river, eastward toward the dusty plains of the caprock, they began to get that funny feeling again.

"Eyes," said Temp.

"Yep," said Bud.

They stopped and looked about until from behind a boulder they heard a belch, followed by a familiar voice, which said, "Sorry." The boys looked at each other and smiled.

"Ain't that nice?" said Temp. "It's Trigger, lookin' after us."

Trigger continued to follow them for several miles, but he never showed himself, preferring to duck in and out of rocks. After a while the boys got used to having him there. It was a safe, protective feeling.

As they crossed into Texas the land changed. The rocks and caves gave way to dust and plains. The sky darkened and the wind gusted. It was then that the funny feeling returned. But this time it wasn't a feeling of being watched. It was a feeling of *not* being watched.

Trigger was gone. They knew it. They were on their own again. Just two brothers, no more.

The wind gusted again and blew a particle of dust into Bud's eye. A moment later, some dust flew into Temp's eye too. The wind grew rapidly fiercer. Soon they could see it twirling on the horizon, and they could hear it howling in their heads. Bud raised his bandanna up over his mouth, got his goggles out of his pack, and motioned to Temp to do the same. Sam let out a shrill whinny, but no one could hear it over the wind.

The horses pressed into the wind as if it were a tidal wave. Every bare inch of the boys' skin burned with the sting of dust. Sam closed his eyes. Seeing couldn't help them now anyway. There was nothing to see. The air was black with dust.

Sam staggered. Bud tried to hold him to a straight course, but he lost hold of the reins. Then, in groping for them around Sam's neck, he lost his goggles too. They fell off into the black nothingness of the dust storm that consumed them—that consumed the caprock.

"Temp," he called, squeezing his eyes tight. He couldn't see; he couldn't even hear himself.

Then he felt a punch at his right arm. He shielded his eyes

and saw that Temp was trying to push his own goggles on
him. Bud shook his head *no* and pushed them back at Temp.
But Temp pushed them back again. "NO," Bud screamed,
but Temp couldn't hear him. "You wear them, Temp. *You.*"

Temp shoved them back at Bud one more time, and this
time he meant it. He handed Bud his reins, pulled his hat down
over his eyes, held tight to the saddle horn, and as Geronimo
lowered his head, let Bud lead them out of the storm.

Bud's only weapon was patience as the horses crept along
agonizingly. With Temp's goggles on he could see about six
inches ahead of himself, but no more. So, six inches at a time,
they shouldered their way through the storm. Quietly, without speaking, numbing themselves to the pain, they stumbled
on and on, not knowing where they were stumbling to.

Nearly six hours later, they rode straight into the side of a
building, which turned out by some miracle to be a livery
stable. Next door there was a hotel, which they found by groping their way along its wall. They bundled themselves up in
their beds, wrapped themselves in blankets, tightly, so that the
dust that blew in through the cracks in the walls couldn't get
them.

When they woke up the next morning, the storm had died
down. Their skin felt raw, as if it had been badly burned. They
walked out onto the road to take a look at the town, but there
was no road there. And there was no town, either. There was
a livery stable and a hotel, all right—they hadn't dreamed

those up. But for miles around—for as far as the eye could see—there was nothing but flat plains and blue sky.

"Reckon someone was looking after us," Bud said. "Someone didn't want to see us lost in the storm."

"Reckon so, Bud."

"Nicest town I've ever seen."

"Yep," said Temp. "Never liked one better."

★ THIRTY-SEVEN ★
Goodnight

It wasn't till noon, after a long, tiring ride, that they found themselves looking at something other than plains and skies. And it was something altogether different from anything they'd ever before seen with their own two eyes.

"Diabalo," said Temp.

"You think it's a mirage?" Bud asked.

"Don't smell like a mirage," Temp said.

"I thought they was all dead," Bud said.

"Can I touch one?"

"I wouldn't risk it," said Bud.

They were about fifty paces away from a herd of woolly, humped, grumbling buffalo, such as the boys thought no longer existed in the West. There had to be at least two hundred head of them.

A few miles farther they spotted a family of pronghorn antelope, their tails flashing like tin pans before they dashed away across the plains. A few miles more and they came to a big ranch house, with a barn nearby and some other out-buildings and several empty corrals.

Outside the ranch house was a white-haired woman talking to some chickens. She cupped her hands around her mouth and shouted into the house, "Goodnight! Goodnight!"

"Why she saying goodnight, Bud, at noontime?"

"It ain't that kind of goodnight," Bud said, his heart pounding with excitement. Then he fell speechless.

When they neared the woman, she said, "Hello, young boys. Will you alight and eat with us? Rusty will take your horses."

A young boy, not much older than Bud, ran out from the barn and took hold of Sam's reins. Bud seemed unsure about what to do, and the fella said, "I ain't gonna *steal* 'em. I'm the horse wrangler. I look after the remuda. Fall off and stay awhile." After the boys had alighted, Rusty dashed into the barn with the horses.

"Goodnight!" the lady called again into the house. "Fly at it!"

The cook came outside and started banging the side of a pot with a spoon. This got about twenty cowboys to come thundering in from the plains, from twenty directions, on twenty beautiful gleaming horses. There were silky-coated bays and midnight blacks, with and without blazes, and dappled grays

and buckskins and pintos. One by one the cowboys hopped out
of their seats and, patting their horses affectionately, waited for
Rusty to run out and relieve them of their mounts.

"That husband of mine is always the last to the table and
the first to leave," the lady said, shaking her head.
"Goodnight!" she called again. With her pet chickens clucking
at her heels, she led the boys to the dining table. "These hens
follow me everywhere," she said, "and they never stop chattering. They seem to think I really do understand them. Of
course, I don't, but the truth is it's nice to have some girls to
talk to."

She put the boys near the head of the long wooden table
and went to get them some food as the cowboys all took their
seats with their plates and coffee mugs in hand. They were
laughing and hungry. Their faces were red from the sun and
their exertions. They were all tall and broad-shouldered, and
they made Bud and Temp feel by comparison like a couple of
little kids.

"What's this?" inquired the first one to notice Bud and
Temp. "Cowboys or schoolboys?"

"Hello, young fellas," another said. "You been long on the
trail?"

"'Bout three weeks and more. Almost four now," said Bud.

"Four weeks!" The men all laughed. "Where from?"

"We've been all around the caprock, down to Roswell, up
to Santa Fe, and over here from Las Vegas," said Bud. "But
home's in Oklahoma."

"Oklahoma?" A low drawling voice drew everyone's attention to the doorway, where there stood a giant of a man, much taller than Jack, with legs so long and bowed so wide apart that Temp could have walked through them on his tiptoes. He was shaking his white shock of hair and saying, grumblingly through a long white beard, "Dang poor recommendation, Oklahoma. Dang poor." Then he spat about a quart of tobacco juice into the dirt before stepping into the dining room and taking his seat at the head of the table, between Bud and Temp.

"Why, Charlie," the lady said, as she took her place, "you know there are many good people in Oklahoma."

"Dang scarce, Mary," he said. "Dang scarce." He nodded to the cowboys and said, "Hello, fellas."

"Howdy, Colonel," said all the cowboys.

Without further ado, everybody began to eat, and not a word was spoken till every morsel was devoured. This took all of about three and a half minutes. Bud could hardly take a bite. He was too nervous to be so near the great Charles Goodnight. When at last he found the nerve to look up from his plate, Goodnight was gone. He'd vanished from his seat.

"Goodnight, Goodnight!" said one of the cowboys, laughing.

After lunch, Bud and Temp rode the horses around the ranch to see the lay of the land. Bud's heart was racing. It was just as he'd imagined it. They went looking for the buffalo again and found them in a high pasture where a stream ran through. Among the humps and woolly backs they spotted a white glowing head. It was Goodnight, on his horse, smoking a cigar and meandering in a dreamy way, weaving in and out among the buffalo.

The boys tried to make the horses walk into the strange herd, but neither Sam nor Geronimo would do it. "Please, Sam," Bud said. "They won't bite." But Sam, who had seen just about everything in his life, had never seen this before, and he wouldn't budge.

Goodnight looked up, saw them, and, with a puff on his cigar, pretended he hadn't seen them. After a while, though, he sighed and shook his head. Then he clucked his tongue and walked his horse over to where Bud and Temp were gaping at him.

"I raised them myself," he said. "Each one, from a baby. Ever seen a buffalo before?" he asked. Both boys shook their heads, *no*. "Well, they ain't never seen two such small cowboys before, either."

Bud was too shy to speak. "Ever see a *cattalo*?" Goodnight asked, to keep the conversation going. "An animal that's half buffalo and half cow? I can show you one."

Temp said, "You're lyin'."

"Am I? You ask Rusty later to show you the cattalo that Colonel Goodnight's been raisin'. And don't call me a liar. Not to my face, anyway." He puffed on his cigar and looked them over. "Who and what are you, anyway? And can the big one speak?"

Bud took a deep breath and said, quiveringly, "We're Louis and Temple, and Jack Abernathy is our father."

"The wolfer?" Goodnight said, his bushy white eyebrows rising sky-high. "You boys crazy like your father?"

"Our daddy ain't crazy!" Temp said. "That's a crazy thing to *say*!"

"Hmm," said Goodnight. "I can see one of you is. What about the other one?" He turned to Bud.

"I'd like to work here, Colonel Goodnight," Bud blurted.

"Oh, would you?" Goodnight said, as Temp shot Bud a look of alarm. "You a hard worker? You know your way around a herd?"

"Yes, Colonel Goodnight."

"Won't your mother miss you?"

"She's dead, Colonel Goodnight."

"Oh," he said, and sighed. "Well, I'm sorry to hear that. But your father's not dead, is he? Last I heard he was still catchin' wolves and outlaws and otherwise being crazy. Surely he'd miss you."

Bud shrugged.

"You good in school?" Goodnight asked.

"I reckon so, Colonel Goodnight. But I don't much want to go back to school." Unbeknownst to Bud, Temp's head dropped to his chest at this bit of news. "Sir, Colonel Goodnight—" Bud continued.

"Young man," he interrupted, "you remind me of the time I got stranded out of town and had to send my wife a telegram, which I wrote down thusly: 'Mrs. Charles Goodnight. Goodnight, Texas. Cannot get home tonight. Goodnight. Charles Goodnight.' Just as the telegraph operator said, as he handed the paper back to me, so I say to you: 'Too dang much Goodnight.'"

Bud looked at him and smiled, and Goodnight smiled back. "I can see you're not crazy like your daddy," Goodnight said, "and that's a good thing. I don't need another wolf-catching daredevil, but I can always use a good, strong, reliable man around the place. I reckon you *could* come here and work, any time you'd like, and I'd be glad to have you. You could start today if you wanted to."

Bud's face lit up. He turned to Temp and was surprised to find him looking so miserable.

Goodnight saw it too. "Why'd you come here, Temple?" he asked. "What were you after?"

Temple shrugged. His lip was quivering a little. "I came to be with Bud," he said, meekly. "'Cause I didn't want to be without Bud."

One of the young buffalo groaned. As Goodnight looked to make sure he was all right, he said to the boys, "Do you know what I don't understand about men?"

"What, Colonel Goodnight?" asked Bud.

"Well, Colonel Abernathy, if you look at a baby alligator, or a young soft-shelled turtle, or a Texas calf, or a little cattaloni, or a wolf pup, or the offspring of every animal there is, except a man-child, you'll see that each of them has an unfailing homing instinct. No matter how far they wander away from the nest, they can always find their way back again. And it seems that as soon as they leave it, it becomes their chief mission in life to get themselves back again. But boys aren't like that, are they?"

"Some are," said Bud. He looked to Temp, worriedly, and saw that his head was slumped to his saddle horn. He was still wearing Bud's old Stetson. And it was still far too big for him. Bud sighed, took one last good look around, and said, "This place—your ranch . . . it's like the West used to be, ain't it?"

"Aw, no," said Goodnight. "A couple hundred buffalo don't change nothin'. The old West is gone, son. It can't come back. The only thing that's the same, thank goodness," he said, lifting his head and letting the breeze blow through his electric-white hair, "is the undying wind. And if that ever stopped, I think I'd fall down and die myself.

"Lots of things is changing fast, everywhere," the colonel said. "*Stink buggies* in the towns, electric lights, folks talking about aeroplanes and such." He shook his head in disgust. "Now, if I was a young boy, I reckon what I'd do is try to see as much of what was left of the natural world as I could, before it was gone forever. And if I had a brother to take with me, one who really needed me . . . why, that would be ideal. It seems you've got a good travelin' partner there."

Bud put his hand on Temp's shoulder, and he squeezed it. "Who, Temp?" he said. "I reckon he'll do to ride the river with."

Goodnight smiled as Temp's spirits began to lift, and he said, "Oh, it's grand to be a boy. Look at you two. You're as free as the wind. Not a care in the world and nothing to fence you in. You boys know your way home from here, don't you?"

"Yes, sir, Colonel Goodnight," Bud said. "Me and Temp don't ever get too lost."

★ **THIRTY-EIGHT** ★

Fly Like the Wind

Home they went, galloping across the Texas panhandle. They enjoyed their last nights under the stars, together. They leaned against Sam and Geronimo for warmth as they ate and slept as near to them as possible so that they could hear their steady breathing. The nights were peaceful. But the days were as fleeting as the wind, and they flew by too fast. Nothing the boys could do would slow down time, forestall the end of their journey, or delay the start of school.

They thundered past the edge of the great Palo Duro Canyon, and then the caprock and their great wealth—one thousand miles—were behind them. Soon they were riding into their own glorious Oklahoma, the youngest state in the union, having earned its place among the forty-five others in the year 1907. On Labor Day, September 6, the day before the start of school, they arrived in Oklahoma City, dusty and tired but happy. They were met there by a brass band playing "There'll Be a Hot Time in the Old Town Tonight." Banners that read "Welcome Home Abernathy Boys" had been hung all about the streets.

Bud and Temp were swept off their horses and onto a fire-truck stage, from which height they waved and bowed as hundreds of people applauded. Bud thought it was a shame that their daddy wasn't there to see all the fanfare. Strangers lifted them into the arms of two men in the crowd, and they were passed overhead, from one man to another, amidst hoorays, until they found themselves standing alone, on the very far side of everything and everybody.

When they landed they saw three women marching toward them, looking as angry as three mad jackasses. Temp grabbed Bud's arm in fear. The largest of them crushed Temple into her bosom and said to the heavens, with the most righteous indignation, "Where is your mother!? Show me the terrible woman who would let you risk life and limb to do this!?"

Temp hardly could breathe, but he managed to make his little muffled voice heard: "My mother's dead, ma'am," he said.

She pushed him away and, holding his shoulders at arm's length, she seemed to melt to pieces. Tears welled up in her eyes. "Poor child," she said. "And your father? Is he dead too?"

"No, ma'am," Temp said. It was at that precise moment that their daddy appeared. He'd arrived late and had just managed to break through the crowd, and just now he'd stepped directly before her, grinning from ear to ear, not knowing what he was stepping into.

"Here he is," said Bud.

"Not dead?! Alive!?" the woman cried in disbelief. She dropped Temp's shoulders, grabbed his father by the vest, and shook him roughly. "You beast!" she said, shaking him. "You beast!"

A few hours' more fast riding, with their father by their side, and they were home and safe. They fed and watered the horses, put fresh straw in their stalls, and stroked their necks for a bit before sitting down to their own meal. After supper, Johnny, little Pearlie, Kitty Joe, Goldie, Dylan, Maxwell, Catch, and their father gathered around them in the parlor and listened to their stories. Catch was delirious at the first sight of them, but after a few minutes he curled up and fell asleep and soon seemed to forget he'd ever missed them.

As their mother's mantel clock ticked, Bud turned everything that had happened to them and everything they saw into shimmering tales that rivaled his father's stories for excitement and wonder.

"We saw everything," said Temp, backing him up. "Everything Daddy told us about. Everything that's good and bad. We saw it. Bud protected us both. He's as good and brave as Daddy. And he only used *one* bullet."

Bud was a little embarrassed by the flattery. "The people were all mighty nice," he said. "Except in Portales maybe, where they were just cranky. We didn't meet any bad men or any outlaws, though. Just good people. That made it easy."

"Didn't Bud do good, Daddy?" Temp asked.

"No outlaws, eh?" answered Jack. He'd been looking at a letter that had come in the morning post. Now he read it aloud: "'To Jack Abernathy: I don't like one hair on your head, but I do like the stuff that is in these kids. We shadowed them through the worst part of New Mexico to see that they were not harmed by sheep herders, mean men, or animals. Signed A.Z.Y.'"

Bud and Temp looked at each other and shrugged. "Don't know any A.Z.Y.," said Bud.

"Temp," said Jack, "you've seen this man's face a hundred times in my office. On a Wanted poster. Long yellow hair in a ponytail. Big smiling mug, sparkling teeth. Born in Arizona. Tried to kill me once. Do you mean to tell me you boys don't know a bad man when you see one? Looks to me like this letter was written with the tip of a bullet. And what I just *can't* believe is that you two let him get away!"

The face of Arizona, alias A.Z.Y., was as fresh in Bud's mind as if he'd seen him minutes ago, not days. An outlaw! Of course he was. It was so clear now. He could see it. The whole trip had gone by so fast and so much had happened. It ought to have been a blur in his mind, and yet it was all crystal clear. The Red River splashing his face. The vaporous mirages changing shapes before his eyes. The wolves blinking at him in the night. Arizona—A.Z.Y.—singing them to sleep. Roswell, the mountains, the dust storm, and Colonel Charles

Goodnight telling him he was in some ways a better man than his daddy. Though he'd never tell his daddy that part.

Tomorrow he'd be back in school with Miss Violet Irene Moore, but this year Temp would be there too. Temp needed Bud to show him around and look out for him. They could bring Ace's Comanche charm, and the drummer's pin, and they could show them to the other kids just to prove they'd really been across the caprock.

If he had to learn his multiplication tables while he was there, then all right, he'd do it. Math and drawing and reading were Miss Moore's philosophies of life, and perhaps they were very good ones, but he had his own to think of too. He'd do his schoolwork, but in his mind he'd be planning his next adventure and dreaming about seeing the country as it was while he had the freedom to do it, being careful next time not to be fooled by outlaws. The mantel clock was ticking. He didn't have all the time in the world. He would do as Colonel Goodnight said: He'd get out there fast, and he'd take his brother with him.